Rhapsody
–in Black–

Rhapsody
–in Black–

J.J. Overton

Published by CRS Publishing
ISBN13-979-8847328012
ASIN: B0BB5Z9DB2

For Sandra David and Chris

Acknowledgements

Grateful thanks to the following people:
Sandra Horton for her patience and her inspiration in helping me write this novel. Thanks to my sons, David and Christopher, for supporting my efforts in novel writing. I also want to thank my friends, Brenden Hindhaugh, Pauline Weston, Heather Harper and Mike Williams, for their encouragement while I wrote *Rhapsody in Black*.

Pond'rous engines clang
Through thy coy dales; while red the countless fires,
With umber'd flame, bicker on all thy hills
Dark'ning the Summer's sun with columns large
Of thick, sulphureous smoke.

Anna Seward; The Swan of Litchfield, 1785.

Chapter 1

1768

Satchwell and Bromwich

Flames illuminated the cobbles through the open door of the forge. Standing in the darkness across the valley of the River Stour, Sam Bromwich could see Elijah Satchwell's silhouette as he worked at his anvil hammering white-hot iron.

Bromwich was curious about the engineer from Cradley who had come into money. Satchwell had taken a risk buying the corn mill. It had been unused for a decade. From the other side of the river, Bromwich watched his neighbour restore the building, converting the old corn mill to a forge mill.

And then, one day, Elijah Satchwell opened a sluice gate. The mill wheel began to rotate, and Bromwich saw a line shaft turning through an open door. Pulleys with leather belts powered a lathe, a milling machine and bellows to force air into a forge.

* * *

Smoke, black and dense, drifted from the chimney stack, and, as his horse needed shoeing and curiosity was getting the better of him, Bromwich arrived at the forge mill.

"I knew you were coming in," said Satchwell. "I saw your shadow on the floor." Elijah Satchwell was a muscular man who looked to be in his thirties. He had an open, friendly face with pleasant laughter lines, and his skin reflected the intense heat of the forge.

1

Satchwell scrutinised his slowly moving tilt hammer, cyclically hitting the anvil. Then, choosing the moment, he placed an oak prop under the hammer to stop its rise and fall. "This damn mill wheel doesn't give enough power."

"Then force more water volume to the mill wheel by changing the flume to Pitchback rather than Undershot. If you do so, you will raise the power of your tilt-hammer almost twofold."

"Is that so?" Elijah's brow puckered as he thought about the advice. And then, "Come, sit down, and we will discuss this." He took two clay pipes off a shelf near the forge, offered one to Bromwich and passed him tobacco. They took a light from the forge, sat and talked.

Sam Bromwich's knowledge impressed Satchwell, and through this casual conversation, a business was formed that would be called the Sampson Ironworks.

* * *

That night, in the cottage adjoining the forge, Elijah sat in his chair more quietly than usual. His temperament sometimes resembled the sparks flying from the red-hot iron he hammered. Sarah gave him a questioning look and put down the book she was reading to their sons, Joseph and the younger boy, Thomas. Elijah told her about his conversation with Bromwich.

"We are starting a business venture, and I wonder how best to proceed."

"What will you accomplish with Bromwich helping?"

"The country will always need food from the fields; farmers want the tools to till the land. So Sam Bromwich and I will forge those tools out of good quality iron to help fill the bellies of the country."

"And the rest of the colonies, I am sure."

Elijah shuffled his feet and looked at Joseph, his older son. "Joss will follow me, and Thomas will help him."

"And the River Stour will pursue us and make us rich," Sarah said, not realising how true her words would be.

The River Stour meandered through people's lives in a once green and pleasant land known in time to come as the Black Country because of coal mines and smoke and fire from forge mills and foundries. The river was ever-present for the people of Halveston because it was there that the Stour grew wide, and its flow was more useful to power the growth of new industry.

* * *

Five years after opening the Sampson Ironworks, Satchwell and Bromwich purchased a steam engine named Leviathan. The water wheel finally stopped, and hissing, clanking machinery drove the line shaft. Men trudged downhill from new terraced houses in the village of Halveston Mill. Instead of working with the cool earth, now they worked with unforgiving iron and steel, feeding the hungry maw of the Industrial Midlands.

Elijah Satchwell's future seemed firmly set, so he employed an architect to design a stately home built of Darley Dale stone. "I want an ornamental pool with a fountain at the rear of the house," Elijah stated. "At the front, there must be a circular arrival area. An archway will lead to a courtyard with stables and a coach-house, and I will call the house Stourton."

Chapter 2

1773

Joss Satchwell

"Father, when I start in the Ironworks, what will I do?" the blond-haired Joseph asked. He was fourteen years of age and was due to start on Monday the following week.

"You will first work with Bill Hammersley in the design shop," Elijah said as they walked by the river. On Sundays, the family would walk along the river from their new house toward Woolford Abbey, where Viscount Adelson lived.

"Where will I work, father?" Tom asked. His features and hair were dark, like his temperament.

"If you are good, you will do the same as your brother. The design shop is where to start. It is where our work begins. The factory gate is where it ends as long as manufacture follows the design correctly."

"But father, I want to work with iron and steel, not with a pencil," the youngster said.

* * *

Bill Hammersley was nervous. He was lying awake that night with his wife at his side. His quietness was unusual, and she summoned the words in the dark and asked what was on his mind, trying not to upset him.

"It is Satchwell's son. He starts work tomorrow in my department. I will be the one teaching him," he said. "It will be no easy feat. But apparently, the boy is keen to learn and will follow his father in the business. The problem is that the boy has a quiet disposition, so to what extent he will have the drive to run the business when it's his turn, I don't know."

"Give it time, Bill. The first day will be awkward, but the lad's skills will become apparent as time passes. Apart from that, your work will be to teach him; it is his responsibility to learn." Adeline's words brought peace to Bill's mind, and he drifted off to sleep.

Before the whistle blew for the start of the shift, Hammersley entered his domain in the foundry. He saw the Satchwell lad standing at the drawing board. The young man looked nervous, not knowing what to do with his hands.

"Good morning, Joseph. And how are you today?"

"I am well, sir," the lad stuttered, picking up a pencil from some lying on a table nearby. He wanted to appear ready for the design task ahead.

"Then we will begin. Joseph, the type of pencil you have in your hand is a recent invention. See the black core?"

Joseph nodded.

"Do you know what it is?"

"I am unsure."

"That type of pencil you hold has the graphite centre in a wooden surround. A German cabinetmaker named Faber invented them. These pencils are useful to us designers because we can easily re-sharpen them with a knife."

Hammersley thought he should address the young man as sir, but he resisted. Elijah Satchwell had spoken to him and said he should deal with his son like any other worker. Bill warmed to the lad, who had open pleasantness to his face.

"While in the design department, those pencils will be one of the major tools you will use, so you must be in command of their capability. In addition, I have found that the graphite's hardness can vary, which is very useful to us."

"How can you tell the hardness?"

"By using the pencils. Keep the hard and the soft separate. Hard is good for outlining and adding dimensional detail to your drawing. Soft is useful for shading."

Joseph nodded.

"Here is a practical test to familiarise you with what these pencils can do. Pick up each of them and sign your name with each one. You will find some are hard and some are soft. Separate hard and soft into those two boxes. And then, with one hard and then one soft pencil, write a paragraph describing the pencils' properties. When you have done that, show me what you have written."

Hammersley left the lad alone and went to his board, where the drawing of a large crankshaft with an adjacent connecting rod was nearing completion. He picked up one of his soft pencils and shaded the connecting rod shaft with geometrically placed lines so that the drawing gained three-dimensional solidity. After a while, Joss finished his task.

"Let me see your work on the board, Joss." Bill picked up a small box from a cabinet at the side of his board and went to Joseph's drawing board.

Hammersley saw neat cursive writing. "You have done well, young man. Your work is excellent." Hammersley handed him the box, which contained a set of drawing instruments. The lad's eyes brightened. "You have potential, Joseph. These instruments will be useful to you. Tell me, what do you know of trigonometry?"

"It is the mathematics of angles, with which I am familiar, and I can use a slide rule to help me compute the angles; and I have learned how to use a Vernier caliper gauge to measure components."

"Have you now? Very well, we will move on. Do your best to measure this valve and draw it in whatever fashion you like, making the scale full-size. You can get the caliper for measuring the valve from the stores."

The years went by, and Joseph reached the age of twenty-three. He had become proficient in the design department, the machine shop and forge work, although design work gave him his greatest satisfaction. The Sampson Ironworks grew in size and advanced in capability, producing iron from ore shipped on the Stour. Satchwell and Bromwich converted iron into steel, and steel was forged and machined into agricultural implements and razor-sharp weapons.

* * *

The family sat at their large dining table. Sarah was at one end, Elijah at the other with his back to a French window. His greying hair was brightened in the darkening room by fiery light from the nearby furnaces. He looked at his sons, aware that each of the young men had different qualities to offer to the growth of the Ironworks.

Apart from unforeseen misfortune, their lives were secure. The large house, Stourton, by the riverside would be their inheritance, and the business would fund the outgoings of the large estate, which boasted a folly in a delightful place accessed through a rhododendron walk.

A maid removed the dinner plates, and the conversation turned to an event that would take place the following day to mark the culmination of Tom's apprenticeship.

"What have you chosen for your apprentice piece, Thomas?" his father asked. Tom marshalled his thoughts. He had considered two objects to mark the extent of his skill, and his temperament fostered the choice.

Sarah looked on expectantly, waiting for Tom's answer. It was rare that she entered the Ironworks. Sarah was concerned with her son's progress, but because of the riches her husband had provided, she had left the simple things of life behind. Her beautiful countenance had hardened. Elijah had no time left in his complicated life to notice the change, so bound up was he with the flow of steel.

Elijah waited for Tom's decision about his apprentice piece. Joss thought the object Tom would make would be a complex agricultural piece for a plough or an edged weapon. Either would show Tom's skill with machinery, an anvil and the forge.

"Thomas, please answer your father. What will you make?" asked his mother.

With the powder keg of youth inside his body and rebellion in his spirit, Tom Satchwell decided what to make because he thought he knew where the future lay.

"I will make a spade," he said.

Joss burst out laughing. Elijah stared at both his sons, trying to understand Tom's choice and Joss's humour.

"What on earth do you want to make a spade for?" Elijah asked.

"Because the earth you've just mentioned is where we come from. Our future years of peace, which will be longer than those captive to war, will lie with the land. Agriculture is the future, father, so I shall make a spade."

Chapter 3

1779

The Forging

When Thomas mentioned the land, Elijah recalled something that happened when he was three. His father had taken him on his shoulders, walking by the river. "This is where we come from, Elijah. We are people of the land and the mill wheel," his father told him. The words had been forged indelibly into Elijah's character

Elijah saw a kindred spirit in Tom, the boy he had previously seen as an intrusion into the progress of the business, with his dark nature and a temper to match. The future had become crystal clear. Tom was the man to lead the business rather than Joseph. Thomas had the needed aggression.

"Make it, Tom. Make the spade with my blessing, and let Satchwell and Bromwich benefit from your foresight. Yes, agriculture is where our future lies. Admittedly, the occasional war will increase our short-term profits. Still, your agricultural tools will be the mainstay of the business."

Joseph's laughter at Tom's decision to forge a spade was replaced with disbelief at his father's confidence in Tom's ability. Joseph's father, mother and brother took no notice as he quietly left the room.

* * *

The last day of Thomas Satchwell's apprenticeship dawned, and he made his way to the steel stores.

"Today is your day then, Master Tom," said Ned Rawnsey.

"My past five years hang on this day, Ned." In one of the steel racks, Tom located the grade of steel with the potential he needed for his project. He could tell its carbon content by the colour code painted on the end of the bar.

"What is it you're crafting, sir?"

"A spade."

"But you've chosen weapon steel."

"I have done that because my spade will thrust at the earth like an enemy, and I will make it to last a hundred years and more. It will leave its mark wherever it goes; mark my words Mister Rawnsey, this will be the spade of all spades."

"Alright, let us part your material from the bar."

Tom took the steel to a forge, placed it in the coke, and forced it to white-hot by bellows driven from the line shaft. The steel quickly absorbed the heat. When it was white hot, Tom grasped it with tongues and took it to the tilt hammer. Strike after strike, it began to thin the billet. Finally, after being reheated and hammered several times, it acquired the spade shape he had planned.

Two men watched silently in the darkness some distance from the fiery work. They saw Tom return the partly shaped spade to the forge and repeat the thinning process several times on the tilt hammer.

"He's almost finished it," Elijah said to Sam Bromwich as Tom went to an anvil with the reheated steel and worked the implement into its final shape by hand. Tom held the spade at arm's length. In the light from one of the furnaces, he admired his work.

It was difficult for the two men watching from the darkness to make themselves heard above the clamour of the tilt hammers and the noise of metal being wrought and machined. Satchwell got close to Sam Bromwich's ear.

"Tom's the one who'll inherit my share," he said. Bromwich looked at him, shrugged, and shook his head. His hearing was poor after his years of foundry work.

"Say again," he shouted.

"I said Tom's the one who will inherit my share," Elijah shouted.

Bromwich shook his head. "You should share it equally."

"I will not." Elijah's stubborn nature surfaced. "Tom can design components in his head, make a prototype and then explain how to draw it. He has both skills; design and manufacturing. Joseph has those skills. He can do better than most, but there the tale ends. He hasn't got the killer instinct needed to battle with our competitors. It is Tom who will run the business." Bromwich was silent. He had heard cruel words and disagreed with them.

Elijah watched with pride as Tom reached into his pocket and took out a metal punch. The young man placed the engraved end onto the front face of the spade socket and struck the punch with a hammer. His initials, *TS,* were impressed deeply into the steel.

"That's his touch-mark," Elijah shouted to Sam. He turned to see his colleague's reaction, but Bromwich had left without speaking.

Joseph had been watching his brother make his apprentice piece. Then, in the darkness, a short distance behind his father and Sam Bromwich, he heard his father's raised voice, praising Tom to the heights of heaven. The cruelty of the words forced anger into Joseph's gentle mind. As tears pricked his eyes, Joss walked away from his father, out of the forge mill.

Joseph looked back at the Sampson Ironworks from the bank of the River Stour. His surname and that of Bromwich were set in an iron arch over the gate into the foundry. The tears dried as Joseph walked toward some woodland on a nearby hill.

Under the canopy of the trees, the birdsong and the coolness, compared to the foundry's heat, helped soothe his mind. He sat on the ground, softened with leaf mould, and re-lived the words he had heard his father shout into Bromwich's ear. Joseph tried to assess his future to gauge how he would fit into the family business. Still, after his father's words, all he could see in the future was emptiness.

His emotions quietened, and a soft breeze caressed his hair, which was the colour of ripened corn.

* * *

Unlike Joseph, Tom Satchwell's future was now indelibly linked to iron and steel. When he leaned the spade against the anvil, his father came out of the darkness to congratulate him on his progress. Thomas had a wayward edge to his thinking. He could not explain why, but sometimes his thoughts rebelled during a conversation. They skittered about, seeking a place to settle. As Elijah came close, his hand extended, Tom's mind saw him as an old fool, a king in his court of iron, eager to pass him the crown and, in time, his fortune. Tom laughed inwardly. He could not care less if he had nothing to do with the Sampson Ironworks. But he wanted the riches, and to get the riches, he had to put up with the iron. Here his father was, offering him everything with wide-open hands and the smile of an old fool.

After Tom made the spade, the brothers were together in the library. The evening began as one of the few times when conversation was easy between them. Then Thomas's attitude changed. He remembered how his father had promised him wealth amounting to a king's ransom. He would be Lord of this manor and send his brother Joseph to damnation for laughing at him when he said he would make a spade as his apprentice piece.

During the past hours, Joseph had come to terms with the fact that he would never have his father's backing. He felt ready to enter an enticing world beckoning outside the foundry. But then, a familiar pattern developed after Tom had drunk too much whisky.

"Friends?" Tom responded after Joseph asked him who he was close to. "I have no friends, nor do I need them." His words slurred together. "Friendships are awkward things. S—so much is demanded and has to be given. I want none of it."

"There is no need to feel like that, Tom. You could have friends if you wanted. People will warm to you if you let them."

"That might be so, but steel is where my heart lies. Father has planned a good future for me here. You . . . well, all you think about is books and your fanciful ideas of things like aerial balloon flight. Your head is in the clouds, Joss. You're as soft as putty." Tom spat out the last words. He stood up, swayed and held onto a chair. "My apprentice piece is pretty well finished. When I am out of my time, I'll have the Sampson Ironworks in the palm of my hand. You laughed at me making a spade. All I have to do is add the ash handle; you and no one else will stop me from finishing it."

"Why would I want to stop you from finishing your spade? The point is, Tom, you are capable of much more. Your skills are such that you could make things of great beauty, and you decided to make a spade."

Tom sat down and rubbed his temples, trying to clear his head from the mist caused by whisky.

"Tom, today, while you were working on the tilt hammer, I heard father telling that man, Bromwich, that he has a fine future for you and that you are the one who will inherit his share of the business."

"Is that so now?" Thomas straightened up and grinned. Joseph saw his brother's features harden, and he tried to bridge the void widening between them with calm words.

"After I heard father speaking today I had anger inside me, so I walked to Ramsdale Hill to clear my mind. Tom, I've decided to go away. I have to get away from this place."

"Well, that's typical of you, soft in the head and a pencil-pushing coward too, u-unable to face father."

In two strides, Joss was in front of Thomas. He grasped his brother's jacket and lifted him from his chair. Tom's face blanched. Joseph's resolve was like the steel he had grown up with and now hated. "Damn you and your attitude, Thomas Satchwell. I am sick of you and father and everything to do with this forge mill. I'll show you who the coward is." He pushed his brother away, and Tom tripped over a rug, landing sprawled on the floor, his head bleeding where it hit the hearth.

Chapter 4

1779

The Journey Begins

"You bloody fool, Joss," Elijah's voice thundered from the doorway. "How dare you do that to your brother in my house?" Elijah offered Thomas his hand to help him up from the floor. But then, words poured out of Elijah that confirmed what Joseph felt.

"You read too much, Joseph. Your Markus Smollett has got to your head with his do-gooding. You talk of William Harris and other such dissenters as if they are God's answer to how we should live and conduct ourselves. Tom has a grip on how we should progress the Ironworks. I will have you know that steel is in our blood, Joss, and I have confidence in Tom that he will lead our production into my grandchildren's future."

"Very well, father, if that is your decision, I'll not stand in your way. But I will tell you this. You must stand by your words. I heard every one of them when you shouted them to Sam Bromwich. You should be ashamed of yourself. So have the steel and your damn forge mill. I hope your riches bring you contentment, but I doubt they ever will."

Elijah looked away from his son. He searched for words to calm the situation but found none.

* * *

Joseph angrily mounted the stairs two at a time, went to his room and surveyed the surroundings. The old familiar things had lost their attraction. He went to the window and looked at the river valley. The glare from the open doors of the furnace halls created a night sky that flickered in the glow of the flames. The River Stour, which had coursed deeply through Joseph's upbringing, was picked out in the crimson light. It tugged at his heart. He loved the river but pushed its influence away, closing the curtain on his life at Halveston.

He took his valise from a cupboard, and put two sets of clothes into it, a razor, some guineas, and silver coinage he had saved up over the years. He opened the door to the landing and listened for movement. There were harsh voices in the library. His father and mother were arguing, and then Tom's voice intervened. Joss heard no detail of the argument, but his mother's share sounded authoritative and unwavering as he silently descended the stairs.

Outside the house, his pace quickened, and he went to one of the terraced houses built for the work people. Then, after a brief conversation with Daniel Makepeace, he headed for the forges.

* * *

Joss knew the routine of the night watchman. The man patrolled outside the works at hourly intervals, armed with a pistol. The watchman's timing was impeccable. Starting on the hour, he entered the engine room. From there, he walked through the forge and each interconnecting workshop, finishing at the Furnace-hall.

In the darkness, Joseph waited for the patrol of the inside of the Ironworks to begin. Then he let himself into the engine room, locking the door behind him. As it was Sunday night, there was no night shift, but oil lamps were still alight, casting a dim glow over the interior of the engine room.

He cautiously entered the machine shop and came to the anvil where Tom had worked on his apprentice piece. There it was, the wrought steel spade with *TS* stamped on the front of the handle socket. Joss picked it up gently. He bitterly regretted knocking Tom to the floor, but he could not draw love from his brother where there was no love to be given. So the next best thing was to take part of his brother with him, the spade Tom had made out of his love of steel.

Joseph heard the night watchman at his work in the Furnace hall. One of his tasks was to keep the furnaces fired, and there was the sound of a shovel scraping coke from a hopper. While the night watchman's work was taking place, Joseph knew he was safe from being discovered.

An ash handle was near the spade. Nearby was a wooden box with a selection of dome head rivets and a hand brace fitted with an awl. Thomas had sanded the handle to fit into the socket, intending to drive in a rivet the next day.

Joseph knocked the handle into place. Where Tom punched two holes in the steel of the socket, Joss drilled a hole through the wood, knocked in a rivet and used a hammer to knock the end into a mushroom shape. He wrapped the spade in some cotton sheeting he had torn from his bed and strapped it to the back of his valise.

* * *

Joseph's friend, Daniel Makepeace, who he had called on earlier, was a quiet-natured lad who could be trusted.

They had become friendly in the drafting office. Joseph drank in moderation at the local inn with Dan Makepeace. On one occasion, they rode together, galloping up the valley of the Stour, looking for its source. They slept under the stars that night and found the river's source at Saint Kenelm's Well, below the hills of Clent.

Dan was waiting at the side of the old header pond, holding the reigns of two horses, not one, as had been the arrangement.

"Why the two horses, Dan?"

"Two horses are needed when two go riding."

"What do you mean?"

"I'm going with you."

"Why? The trouble with my father shouldn't affect you."

"I wouldn't go because of your problem, Joss. I'm going because I need a change for myself. Your departure is a good opportunity to do that."

They rode to where the Stour had its confluence with the River Severn at Stourport upon Severn. After breakfast at an inn, they went to the recruiting sergeant of the 64th Regiment of Foot.

* * *

Joseph Satchwell was third in the queue, and Daniel was fourth. The recruiting sergeant rolled his eyes and smiled when he heard the Satchwell name and realised that Joss was the son of Elijah Satchwell, the steel baron.

"I don't give a damn who you are, sir. Don't think being your father's son will get you any favours."

"I don't want any favours."

"Very well. I shall remember that. What is your age, Master Satchwell?"

"Twenty and three years, sir."

"Don't you sir me . . . sir. At least, not yet. Anyway, Master Satchwell, can you write your name?"

"I can."

"Then, if you want to fight for the King in the American Colonies, sign here; if not, goodbye and get on with your life. But if you intend to sign, I want to know what that thing is on your back."

"My possessions are in the valise. I have a spade, which is dear to me. It will be useful, sergeant. Give me the pen, and I will sign." Joseph dipped the pen and signed. It was a proud signature with a flourish at the end.

Chapter 5

1782

An Anthem for Lost Youth

Two years passed since Joseph signed the ownership of his life over to the King. His home was a distant memory unless an event, or maybe a scent or a sound, brought it sharply, sometimes painfully, to mind.

For a month, fighting had been fierce for the men on loan from the 64th Regiment of Foot under the command of Sir Henry Clinton. Then, finally, the regiment transferred to the southern theatre of operations. Joseph and Daniel were holed up with men they had trained with behind a forward line of breastworks from where they surveyed Charlestown.

Volleys of musketry, which had been intense for half an hour from both sides, ceased. Joseph felt the barrel of his rifle. It had been hot but soon cooled in the break from fighting.

"Listen to that,"

"What is it you hear?" Dan Makepeace cocked his ear in the direction Joseph was pointing. Gunfire had affected his hearing, and he had difficulty hearing Joss's voice, let alone what he had heard.

"It is a nightingale, I am sure," Joseph's voice was quiet.

"It may be, but we are far from hearing that little beauty on a peaceful evening in England. Will you write some lines about him?"

"I have some in mind. There it is again. The song reminds me of home."

"Now that's a fine thought in this God-forsaken place, Joseph Satchwell." The shooting started again from behind a wall held by the Americans a hundred yards away. Daniel ducked as a ball hissed overhead.

"Yes, but I long to be back in England, where I could walk by the river," Joseph said, leaning close to Dan's ear.

Dan rammed a wad home onto the powder charge and then a ball. "Come and taste this, you rebels," he shouted and fired. He saw the ball's impact on the stonework to the right of the man who was his target.

"Is that the best you can do?" the Englishman to Dan's left called.

"It's not as good as I can do," Joseph said. He had heard the birdsong again and imagined himself back on the bank of the Stour, walking along its greenest parts, well away from the new industry, and he wanted to be there. A volley of shots rang out from behind the wall in Charlestown. But the musket shots were inaccurate and thudded into the ground away from the British forward line.

"This is how it should be done," Joseph shouted as he scrambled up the parapet. Daniel grabbed his ankle, pulled, and shouted for Joss to get down, but he shook himself loose, and the warm breeze and sun caught his blond hair and teased it, like it used to do at home. Then, wanting to hurt no one, Joss aimed his rifle at the wall and pulled the trigger. As the ball raised dust from the stonework, he thought he heard laughter from one of the rebels.

"Father!" Joseph shouted as a shot rang out from a hundred yards away and found its mark.

* * *

Daniel Makepeace used the spade Joss had brought from home to dig his grave. Joss had never said much about the spade, but he always had it with him and treated it as something precious.

"Oh, Joss, what have you done?" Dan said, the tears falling as he knelt by the mound of earth. The place was special with his friend buried beneath it, and Daniel wanted to stay with him, but the truce for burial was over, and the tumult of war with its utter futility began once more.

1788

Five years had passed since the end of the war. Charlestown had been renamed Charleston. Independence from the British Empire had been accomplished, and the destruction wrought upon the town had largely been repaired. Near what had once been a defensive redoubt outside the town, there was a pleasant spinney of young red maple trees. They gave the ground below them a peaceful shade, but the red colour of their fallen leaves also gave the land the colour of spilled blood.

A slight mound was almost indiscernible with the settling of the disturbed ground. This faint evidence marked the remains of Joseph, the young man with a gentle nature. In the worst of times, Joss called for his father, longing to be home on the bank of an English river.

Chapter 6

1791

The Botanist

Two British merchant ships, Aurelius and Dragonfly, carrying rolls of woven cotton with a Manchester stamp, hove to off-shore at Charleston in the late morning. The crew were at ease after the long voyage from Liverpool, and boats were lowered and rowed, taking them to the steps of a jetty, where they could hear the sound of revelry coming from the Rubicon Tavern.

George Perceval, captain of the Aurelius and senior to the captain of the Dragonfly, climbed the steps, grasping a hand rope because the growth of seaweed made the steps slippery. Perceval was met by the harbour master and James Donovan, a customs official. Perceval handed paperwork to Donovan, who called a group of stevedores to unload the cargo into a dockside warehouse.

Dragonfly's Captain, James Howard and all but a skeleton crew who remained aboard the two merchant ships scrambled up the harbour steps and headed for the Rubicon Tavern. One of the men, Benjamin Lawrence, was a botanist and newly married. And as the Rubicon Tavern's fame concerning all manner of vices had spread far further than Charleston, Ben was guarded about going there. All he wanted was to drink refreshing ale after so long at sea.

Ben Laurence was a botanist and an artist with an exceptional eye for detail using pen and watercolour wash. His thoughts revolved around roots, rhizomes, petals, stamens and anthers, and his beautiful wife.

An offer had been made to Laurence to join the crews of Aurelius and Dragonfly on the freight mission, which, after cargo delivery, would become an expedition paid for by Sir Joshua Russell. The two ships would proceed to Southern America to search for specimens of the genus Orchidaceae and seek out new flora and fauna.

Benjamin Laurence's botanical drawings won the acclaim of Sir Joshua Russell. He viewed them before an exhibition at the Royal Academy of London, which had the patronage of King George the Third. Due to the sheer accomplishment of artistry, Laurence's paintings were exhibited on the eye-line rather than being hung higher. William Pitt the Younger had accompanied the King to the exhibition. Both paused before the explanatory text and beautifully crafted botanical watercolour of the Jacobite Rose, Rosa Alba Maxima.

"Is that painting a challenge, sir, would you say?" asked the King of his Prime Minister. Pitt the Younger was astute and a diplomat as much as a politician. He knew how to ensure his role as premier stayed secure.

"Sir, it is not a challenge for the artist. On the contrary, it is a work of art that shows considerable talent." Pitt was tempted to touch the painting and feel the artist's contact with the rose, but he resisted.

The King touched it. "Who is this artist?' he asked as he bent to read the signature, holding a pair of spectacles near the painting to magnify the name. A voice from behind said, "If it pleases Your Majesty, the artist is Ben Laurence; he is with us here and at your service." The King recognised the voice of Sir Joshua Russell, the naturalist, who was also a friend with whom he had sponsored expeditions to distant and savage lands in search of interesting botanical specimens and new life forms.

"Where is Benjamin Laurence? Come here, sir," the King shouted. "We wish to meet you."

Laurence had to push through the crowd, who made way for him when they knew he was the artist. When he reached the King, the onlookers burst into spontaneous applause. They had recognised a great artist by his splendid work. Laurence bowed slightly before the sovereign, who was momentarily distracted.

"One minute, Laurence. Where is Sir Joshua Russell? Damn me, Russell; please approach us, sir, will you." Russell was forty-six years of age. He was popular and influential, much respected by his contemporaries for searching the World for curiosities. The King stepped aside so that the conversation would be between himself and Russell alone.

"Sir Joshua, the current expedition is almost ready to sail, is it not?"

"Indeed it is, sir. The two ships, Aurelius and the Dragonfly are but four days from leaving Liverpool port. Remaining provisions needed for the expedition should be reaching the quayside for loading tomorrow."

"Are they armed? The French are untrustworthy at present."

"Both are sloops, third-rate ships of the line with sixteen cannon each."

"And your people of science who are to accompany the expedition, are they prepared, and are they able?"

Russell could see where the question was leading and bent to the King's suggestion. "It would be useful to have a man with such talent as Ben Laurence on board ship, sir. Would you like me to approach Laurence on the matter?"

"Please do, and with some urgency due to your schedule for embarkation. Laurence will serve our nation well."

Ben Laurence was honoured to have been approached by the King through Sir Joshua Russell. That evening, after the doors of the Royal Academy closed and darkness descended upon the works of art, Laurence conversed with his wife in their rented apartment. Jane was proud of her husband; she was well aware of his prodigious talent and how far it could take him, and she intended to ensure his progress.

"I will miss you so much, Ben, but this is a rare chance; you should take it. Our love is strong and can bear the parting."

"But it could be for two years or even longer."

"Our love will be all the stronger when we are together again," Jane said. Her emotion was mixed. She wanted to be with her husband of not many months. But she recognised that the fame and fortune that could come with a successful expedition would provide them with the financial means to ensure no food shortage or struggle for lodgings for the rest of their lives.

On the next day, when the cries of London traders had barely sounded, Ben and Jane began to search the shops for a sea chest. Finally, they found one with steel bands and an arched top. It would be large enough for clothes, tools, pigments, brushes, pens, inks and paper, and the accoutrements of a botanist.

The whole affair had been rushed. The passage of time from recognition by the King to weighing anchor had been only four days. But nevertheless, there had been a night of romance that would remain in the memory of Jane and Ben Laurence until they grew old and their eyes grew dim and finally closed.

* * *

Half an hour after the Aurelius and Dragonfly crews entered the Rubicon Tavern in Charleston, the atmosphere became lewd and indecent. One of the Dragonfly's crew, an Irishman, Seamus O'Hare, nudged Ben's arm when a dark-haired Mulatto woman began a suggestive dance to the guitar of a man she came with into the tavern. Ben felt his colour rise. He stepped away from O'Hare and headed for the door. He was damned if he would get involved with the events that were bound to follow.

"Hey, where are you going, clever boy," O'Hare called after him. "Come back and enjoy the fun." The Irishman's voice was loud and already slurred with the drink. Ben ignored the taunt, shouldered the double swing doors open and stepped outside into the cool air.

O'Hare lurched after him, accompanied by the jeers of the crew of the Dragonfly. This response failed to get the backing of the crew of the Aurelius because an air of competition existed between the two ships' crews. The crew of the Dragonfly followed O'Hare out of the Rubicon onto the wooden sidewalk.

"Hey you," O'Hare called after Laurence, who stopped but didn't turn around. Instead, he waited to see what the Irishman intended to do. He knew O'Hare was worse for drink, but the threat was real. Ben heard him shuffling unsteadily, drawing near to him on the sidewalk.

"Watch out, Ben, mind your back," called Geoffrey Buck, who, by chance on the voyage, was one of Ben's colleagues from Christ Church College. Ben turned and faced O'Hare, who was three paces away, grinning.

"What do you want," Ben asked.

"I want to see you and your kind licked to a pulp."

"Do you now?"

O'Hare edged closer.

"Go on, Seamus, give him and his kind a farewell ticket," shouted one of the Dragonfly's crew. Which was when Ben Laurence leapt forward and gave O'Hare a straight right on the chin, putting him on the floor.

"Do you want any more, Seamus?" asked Laurence, his voice sounding cultured. "I will give you more if you want, but I will tell you this, don't enter my territory again without permission." The crew of the Aurelius had silently gathered behind Laurence, and they did not appear friendly.

O'Hare staggered to his feet. "I'll get you for that, Laurence."

"Oh yes?" Ben approached O'Hare again, and the man turned around and walked away, going back through the swing doors into the Rubicon.

The crews dispersed, making their way back into the tavern. Ben heard the Second Mate of the Dragonfly speaking to Captain Perceval, "That has quietened him, sir. On our voyage, when we were neck and neck in our race for the lead, O'Hare said we should fire a broadside into Aurelius. He is a bad influence on our expedition."

"O'Hare is a troublemaker. He will be put in irons or left

here in Charleston; I can assure you of that."

* * *

Charleston still bore strong marks of the rebellion against colonialism. Battle-scarred houses had changed hands, sometimes by exchanging a bullet, and now the owners of the properties had American accents, not English. Business was thriving. There were shops where enterprising people had seen the need to supply goods they had made or grown, which they sold to the republican population.

Ben Laurence and Geoff Buck strolled down the wooden sidewalk in a broad thoroughfare. They came to a store selling ironmongery, old and new, all still useful. Hanging on the wall behind the counter were handguns and muskets. Weapons were needed by men, women and entire families preparing to venture into the wild and savage country away from townships. Other hardware was lying in boxes, on shelves and propped against the walls.

A spade attracted Ben's attention. The face of the blade reflected the sunlight. He picked it up and touched the steel, feeling oil protecting its surface. In the brief time available to prepare for the expedition, he had packed a trowel, a hand fork, secateurs, and grafting knives in a roll of hessian but ran out of time to get a spade.

He took it to the counter. "How much is this spade?" He asked the bespectacled proprietor. His shop being close to the quayside, the shopkeeper was used to customers with accents that were difficult to understand. Most of the seagoing customers bought weapons.

"That will cost you a Dollar, sir. It is good steel; you can tell by the sound. Here, tap the blade with this." The proprietor handed Laurence a small cold chisel, and when he tapped the spade, the blade rang with a clear bell-like tone. Ben noticed two marks stamped into the front face of the socket holding the handle. He brushed away some caked mud and the remnant of a red leaf and saw the letters T and S stamped into the metal.

Chapter 7

1792

The Southern Continent of America

Twenty-six days after the Aurelius and the Dragonfly left Charleston, they dropped anchor in the forested estuary of a great river where they would be protected from the open sea. The freshwater flowing out of the estuary at a moderate speed was reddish-brown due to the sediment it carried. Staying true to his profession, Benjamin Laurence recorded all events of significance in a journal, along with sketches.

'We have moored in the estuary of a great river that I am sure is the one Sir Joshua required us to locate, known as Amazonas. The topography accurately follows the early map of the region produced by Nicolas Sanson and the recent cartographical work of the explorer Charles Marie de La Condamine. We have located a friendly settlement on the Northerly shoreline, and we have traded baubles with the people who speak a language based on Portuguese.

'After loading supplies, we will proceed inland along the Amazonas as far as the draught of the ships will allow. From that point, we will venture inland to fulfil the purpose of our mission, to look for, record, and obtain specimens of the genus Orchidaceae. There is great demand for these plants in England. Sometimes one plant can realise as much as twenty guineas.'

* * *

They made their way up the river and dropped anchor early one evening when the clearance between the keel and the river bed had reduced to an average of two fathoms. The shoreline was wild. Trees with massive roots grew to the edge of the water. Sunlight low in the west spread an amber afterglow and put the canopy of the trees into a dark profile.

Ben Laurence was on the foredeck in conversation with Captain Perceval. Perceval had been with James Cook on the expedition when Captain Cook was murdered. Perceval was a rough and ready character, well-chosen as the senior officer of the expedition because of his relaxed leadership. He got to know Ben Laurence early in the voyage. Laurence's credentials made him the chief naturalist of the journey, and it had become an evening ritual for him and the captain to review the expedition's progress.

"That is a wild shoreline, Ben. What lies beyond the trees where the river laps their roots; what say you?"

"Our imaginings can be fanciful at the going down of the sun when the light carries an air of mystery. We have an alien shore before us, Captain. Darkness is an hour away; listen, the creatures of the night are at their preparation."

"The sounds make me uneasy. However, I will be abed in the comfort of my cabin less than an hour from now. The noise of the wilderness will be quietened with the help of a few measures of the King's grog. The cannons are primed and ready. And you, Ben, our man of letters, what do you plan for the morrow?"

"According to La Condamine's map, a Northerly inlet is a few miles upstream. He ventured into the inlet for half a day. Before he turned back, he noticed great crags of rock bestrewn with colour beyond the trees. I want to take two of the ship's boats with six armed men each, and we will explore that region and obtain samples."

"Well done, Ben. They will sell for a handsome profit. We have empty holds. Fill them with precious cargo."

* * *

The sound of oars rhythmically entering the water and clunking in the rowlocks added a false tranquillity to the surroundings. The noise of unknown life in the jungle pressed in upon the occupants of the two boats.

Ben Laurence was in the bow of one of them, taking notes and making brief sketches as they progressed. His colleague, Geoffrey Buck, also with a sketchbook, was busy in the bow of the second boat. Suddenly, with a curse, Buck used the sketchbook to swat at the cloud of insects following them. Buck tended to be short-tempered, and the tense feeling created by the jungle and the dense undergrowth brought his bad mood to the surface.

La Condamine's reported distance was accurate, and the time he had spent travelling up the inlet must have been at a similar pace to the Laurence journey. Half a day had passed when, rounding a bend where the trees hung low overhead, a burst of colour could be seen on the river bank to the right. As they drew level with it, they could see high crags of rock covered in foliage, which sported outcrops of riotous colour. The musky scent of the flowers hung heavily in the air.

The area of water in front of this remarkable scene was sufficiently clear of forest debris to allow the two craft to draw close to the bank. Then, taking care that no predatory creatures lurked nearby, the men disembarked.

The soil at the foot of the crag was soft, warm, and sheltered by rocks and trees from storm and wind. The specimens of Orchidaceae growing in profusion were unrecognisable to the botanists.

"This is a treasure-trove of new varieties," Geoffrey Buck's voice was trembling with emotion, his fit of temper forgotten. "These are in an ideal location."

"True; look at those beauties." Ben pointed to the specimens near the rock face. He dug up one of the plants, placed it in a sample box and covered half of its rhizomes with its native soil. Then, he stood, straightened his back and rested his spade against the crag.

"I would recommend this make of spade, Geoff. It will last me all the time I need it."

"Let me see." His colleague examined it. It was unusual because the blade had been sharpened at the tip and halfway up its length. Geoffrey thrust it into the soil to obtain another specimen of orchid. The flower was flame-red and cream with small tan-coloured spots, and each sepal had a near-black border. He teased the plant from the soil and was prepared to hand the spade back to Ben when a slight movement in a tree above Ben's head caught Geoff's attention. Hanging from a branch was a brightly coloured snake. Mouth open, its gaze fixed and predatory.

"Hold still." Geoff's command was sharp enough to stop Ben from moving. He glanced up slowly, following Geoff's gaze.

"Oh, damn," he said quietly, keeping still. The snake was banded, red-brown, white and black. Ben's instinct told him it was dangerous. The more colourful the snake, the more venomous it was. He froze, and his thoughts immediately turned to his young wife, her love of him, her beauty, and his love for her. In that brief moment of a dire threat, he recalled saying he loved her more than she loved him. *'No, you don't. I love you more,'* she said, and they laughed.

Geoffrey's thoughts were far from sentimental. He recognised the snake as one of the most venomous species. He also knew that he was holding a weapon. One of Geoffrey's pastimes had been fencing with the epée, a heavy-bladed sword used to inflict the most damage to an opponent, even decapitation if used in battle.

Geoffrey slowly lifted the spade and gauged where he would cut. The snake began a mouth-open side-to-side movement, setting Ben as its target. Then, with a wild release of energy, Geoffrey swung the spade as he would at an enemy.

Many specimens of flora and fauna were collected and stowed in the hold of the Aurelius and the Dragonfly. With the amount of interest in such rare plants amongst the nobility and industrialists of Great Britain, the financial outlay of the expedition would be well covered.

The holds housed live specimens too. Collections of winged insects. Creeping things with many legs. All manner of reptiles slithered in glass cases.

Part of the expedition's profit would be shared amongst the crew. So, despite a period of foul weather and mountainous seas, the mood of the men remained buoyant. Aurelius and Dragonfly made good progress. They were going home.

Chapter 8

1794

The Homecoming.

Arrangements for the homecoming had been hurried. The communication was by letter carried by a sweating packet captain on horseback, who conveyed it to Sir Joshua Russell and thence to the Duke of Norfolk, who organised all public affairs. The Duke took the letter to the King.

"Get the welcome organised. I tell you, this must be a very public affair. Swags and banners must be displayed, and the band of the Coldstream Guards will play as the ships reach the dockside."

"Yes, your majesty. All of this is necessary because of the expedition's success, but the time we have left to arrange it is short."

"Then commence, Charles. Don't tarry, my Lord of Norfolk."

"What do you suggest the Guards should play?"

"Use your imagination, Charles. Do I have to tell you everything? I suggest a lively piece—something stirring. Rule Britannia may be appropriate. Now go, sir. Time is short, so commence your work."

* * *

Dark clouds of unrest were on the horizon. In France, bloodshed and chaos reigned. Since 1789 heads had been falling, and blood flowing in the gutters was a formality. Louis XVI had been sentenced to death.

Fear was in the air in London. The dissent in Paris was rippling across the English Channel. Those who possessed much were frightened that those with little might attempt to alter the situation by force, as they had in Paris.

That the British have-nots might do the same as those in France was worrying for those with plenty. The storming of the Bastille was a turning point in France. It proved to the field workers, street sweepers, manual labourers, and others who called themselves the Sans-culottes that they did not have to be submissive to those oppressing them.

However, welcoming heroes back home from expeditions to new lands was a diversion to give to the people of England that would promote optimism. The men of science, invention and engineering were valuable. If bright inventiveness kept occurring and steel, iron and brass in new and exciting shapes issued from foundries and machine shops of the middle shires, a revolution would occur by industrial growth, not by blood swilling in the streets.

The weeks of the voyage home passed uneventfully for the botanic artist, apart from an encounter with an albatross that some of the crew thought was the devil incarnate. They believed that the scavenger of the seas was the bringer of ill fortune. Ben Laurence memorised the vision of the bird on the wing. Then, in the evening, controlling his brush with difficulty because of the ship's rolling, he painted a scene of the creature gliding near the masthead, wings outstretched before a fierce sky.

* * *

A cry arose from a sharp-eyed twelve-year-old lad standing on an upper foretopsail yard of the barque, St. Just, moored alongside a West Indiaman.

"They're here, yonder, just at the bend in the river," he shouted. He scuttled down the ratlines preparing to get close to the explorers. Jed Tanner had dreams about ships and far-flung lands full of mystery.

The Aurelius and the Dragonfly were towed in turn by a tug belching black smoke to a position where there would only be a short row in the ships' boats to the harbour steps.

Ben Laurence climbed unsteadily up the steps looking for Jane. During the final leg of the journey from Liverpool to London, she had occupied his mind constantly. As a result, he had difficulty finalising his notes and artwork into manuscript form for submission to the publisher.

At the top of the steps, Laurence saw the swell of people, a colourful cheering mass of humanity, living their excitement to the background of a military band playing Rule Britannia near a five-storey warehouse. And then Ben saw Jane pushing her way swiftly through the crowd as if her life depended upon it. He dropped his valise, which clanged onto the dockside; he didn't care about the equipment. As far as he was concerned, for the time being, it was done with.

"Jane," he called, and then she was with him, held in his arms, her and a child.

"She's ours, Ben, our daughter."

"A daughter, oh Jane, what is she called?" He looked into the little girl's eyes, which were brown and beautiful, like her mother's eyes. The child was smiling.

"She is Lucy. Lucy, this is your father."

"Lucy . . . oh Lucy Laurence, how pretty you are, just like your mother." Ben held them both tight. "Jane, I shall never go away again."

And then Lucy Laurence said, "Hello, daddy," just as her mother had taught her.

* * *

Young Jed Tanner saw the opportunity. He was a chancer, an opportunist. A rough-life survivor, living in Spitalfields with his family in one room, divided for privacy by curtains. A group of people were approaching the men who had disembarked. Jed recognised one of the men, who had his face on the sovereign he had acquired from a gentleman's pocket.

"Well, blow me up. It's bloody George, upon my life," Jed said as he reached for the spade tied loosely to some baggage. The spade caught in the ties, and Jed bent down quickly to correct the problem.

A second, and it was in his hands. Jed had a good teacher, a man of the streets known as Wishbone; he went this way and that way; no one knew his real name. Jed's eyes flicked around; no one caught on. He ran as fast as the wind, clutching his find, dodging in and out of the spectators.

Chapter 9

1794

Jed Tanner

Jed Tanner's home was in a room up three flights of stairs on Spitalfields' Sclater Street. Urchin was the word that most aptly described Jed. Born within the sound of the bells of St. Mary-le-Bow made Jed a true Cockney. He was a tousle-headed lad, always in third-owner clothes that were out at the knee and elbow. He was more often than not without boots because he was more comfortable barefoot. But his eyes . . . those blue eyes set in a handsome face could make a girl's heart flutter. Even the older girls commented about Jed Tanner's eyes; some wished he was their age.

The room Jed and his family called home was empty when he arrived with the spade and some baubles he had lifted out of the pockets of the unsuspecting. He rested the spade against a wall, which had a grimy window overlooking Sclater Street, and emptied the oversized pockets of his jacket onto a deal table under the window. Amongst the items were a piece torn off a loaf and four apples. After dividing the bread into four, Jed placed an apple and some bread on the table by each chair.

Jed heard his mother, Ruth's light footsteps and those of Rebecca, Becky, his sister of eight years, coming up the stairs. Becky was always cheerful, even when she was hungry, which was often. His mother was often tired after washing and wringing dirty water from clothes. Her hands were sometimes painful, cracked and tender due to the hours she spent laundering. Jed wished he could do something about it and vowed that he would.

His mother saw food on the table.

"Oh, Jed, you got us something to eat. You didn't get into trouble, did you?"

He wouldn't be home if he had got into trouble, but she was his mother. She was concerned about him and was glad food was on the table.

"Shall we wait until dad comes back?" said Becky. She was a thoughtful girl. In years to come, Becky would be a good wife. Even in her tender years, she had the compassion to think about the other person rather than herself.

Jed looked at his mother's hands. In some places, they were raw, with blood showing. Then, without being asked, he went to the cupboard and took out the tub of goose grease and beeswax salve made to his grandmother's recipe. The ointment helped when his mother's hands were particularly sore.

When he was applying the ointment, his mother drifted off to sleep.

"Is she alright?" Becky whispered.

"She is tired after her day's work. This will help. He finished with his mother's hands and wiped his own hands on a scrap of cloth.

* * *

In the early evening, the door into the garret opened, and a pleasant-faced man came in. Sometimes when his father came in late, he would look bruised. This time he had a bruised cheekbone. On these occasions, he looked older than his years. Still, the rent was in arrears, and the landlord had threatened eviction, so extra work was necessary to provide for his family. Jed's father, Adam, was hard-pressed in manual labour. On some occasions, Jed thought, this showed on his face.

"What's that?" Adam pointed to the spade.

"A spade," Jed said.

"I know it's a spade. What I mean is, where did it come from?" Adam went to the spade and picked it up. He saw the way it had been forged and finished. "This was made by an expert craftsman." Before the downturn in his fortunes, Adam Tanner had been a mould-maker involved in making moulds for casting ironwork for bridges and roof supports.

"Do you think it's a good day's work, dad?"

"Probably more than you realise, Jed. You may have risked everything to get it, but it has bought us the chance we need.

"What do you have in mind, Adam?" asked Ruth.

"The Grand Junction Canal. Labour is needed to dig the Cutting, and those employed must provide their own tools. I could not afford to buy a spade because of our debts, but here is a spade, and it's a good one. Providence has dealt us a good hand at last. Jed, you are a good, resourceful boy and a thief. But with this spade, we will get you out of thievery." Adam looked around the dismal room. He noticed Ruth's hands, how sore they were; he went to her and kissed her gently, took her hands in his, and looked at his son.

"Jed, you have set us on the road out of this place. Thank you, son."

* * *

They started that evening, each taking possessions

rolled in cloth, hung from the end of a stick resting on the shoulder. Adam Tanner had the spade slung across his shoulders on a leather strap. On the walk from Spitalfields to Uxbridge, where the Cut was being dug, Adam told his son how they would work. Adam was sure he would get employment, the need was great for workers, and the landed gentry, who invested a great deal of money in the project, were not too particular about who did the work as long as it was done on time and within their cost restraints.

"As I see it, Jed, I will do the manual labour; you will be at my side to supply me with food and drink."

"Will I dig as well?"

"Sometimes, to help build up your muscles, but we want you to have no injury, so you must be careful."

"Where will we get food and drink?"

"We will find out what the workmen do for food, but you will take no chances, Jed. The art of pocket-thievery you have become so good at in the busy streets of London will not be needed now. We'll earn enough money for you to forget that way of life."

Jed Tanner's way of life had been that of survival. Thievery was all he had known in his short life. Helped by the tuition of the Wishbone, Jed had struck out on his own. This strange apprenticeship had benefited him and his family, but it was dangerous. It could be hanging by the neck or deportation-dangerous.

"I will give you some of my wages as an allowance to buy what we need," said his father. "The rest of the money will go to your mother."

"How will mother get the money?"

"You will take it to her. You must remember this route we are using, Jed; you will use it often."

"What will it be like when we get to the Cut?"

"I don't know, but I have heard tales that it is difficult work. Sometimes the men are unruly and spoil for a fight, especially when the drink is in them on pay-day."

"Can you fight, dad?"

"I can. There are things your mother and I have not mentioned to you. We will talk about those things now we have time together."

"Do you have secrets then?"

"Son, I have had to earn money to help us survive, and I do that in various nameless places."

"What do you do?" Adam was silent for a few paces. Clouds were gathering. He looked at the sky and hoped the rain wouldn't start while they were walking. He felt Jed looking at him, waiting for his answer about where he spent some of his evening hours.

"I am a fighter, Jed. I am known as Dick Hammer."

"You are Dick Hammer?" Jed had heard of the pugilist. He was well known in London for his defence over forty rounds and bursting with energy when his opponent was exhausted after trying to break through the defences.

Jed looked up at his father and saw him in a new light, as a man trying to battle his way out of the station in life they were in to get them into something better. Jed was no mean scrapper himself. He sometimes arrived home bloodied and tidied himself up before the others arrived.

"Can you teach me to fight as you do, dad?"

"I may."

Jed now understood why his father occasionally looked bruised. They trudged on. Jed's right foot had begun to hurt. He stooped down and unlaced his boots. He tied the laces together, hung them around his neck and nodded to his father that it was alright to carry on.

It was dark, and they were finding their way by the light of the Moon. The air was growing chill.

"There is a light ahead. We must soon find somewhere to bed down for the night. If that is a coaching inn, we might find shelter in the stable or one of the outhouses. We don't want to be out all night. The stars are clear now, and there is a bright quarter moon. There will be a frost."

Under the sign of the Four Feathers, Adam could see a cobbled courtyard through an archway wide and tall enough for a carriage to pass through. There was an outbuilding and a stable where horses could be heard moving on the left of the courtyard. On the right, a carriage was at rest.

"That coach will not be leaving before the day's begun," Adam whispered, "It's our shelter for the night." They hugged the wall, climbed into the coach through the door in darkness, and were soon asleep.

Adam awoke as the sky was showing the first sign of light. He nudged Jed, and they crept away from the shelter of the carriage and resumed their trek.

By mid-day, they were aware of noise in the distance. "It's the Cut workings we can hear," Adam said. "When we arrive, say nothing, leave the talking to me and don't get it into your head to investigate pockets." He looked at his son, who laughed. "I mean it, Jed. We need a good start with our enterprise."

Chapter 10

1794

The Cut

In Maytime, the Cut had progressed to Uxbridge. Jed Tanner and his father came to where lock gates were being hung. The gang foreman directed Adam and Jed to a site office a mile down the Cutting.

They passed by a scene of industry that defied imagination. Men with wheelbarrows full of soil guided them up embankments on planks as donkeys pulled them up to the top. And then the process began again. It was endless but regular work with good pay. Shovels, spades and pickaxes were being wielded. In another area, cattle were being driven along the Cut, consolidating clay laid on the ground to make the canal impervious to Thames water when the coffer dam was raised at Brentford.

"I've counted over four hundred men working the Cut on our way here," Adam said as they drew near where the work was busiest.

"Will they have room for us?"

"Bound to have. Building the Grand Junction Canal is the largest project ever undertaken, and the call for labour is still country-wide." Adam shifted the spade on his back to relieve his shoulders.

The office was a temporary affair, which could be dismantled and moved onward as the Cut progressed. They approached the hut and, through a window, saw an oil lamp illuminating the interior.

"Enter," boomed a voice from within after Adam's knock. They entered the hut, where three men stood around a table studying a large plan on paper curled at the edges.

"Sir, I trust we have come to the correct place. We are looking for employment."

"Are you now," boomed the voice of a man wearing a tricorn hat. "The hiring man is in the office a hundred yards from here. It is Henry Sawyer you need to see. Now go, for we are busy."

"William, hold; the man and boy are tired," said a cultured voice from the shadows at the back of the room. "Put down your baggage and rest. You look to be done in." George Nugent-Temple-Grenville, Marquis of Buckingham, an investor in the canal project, came forward.

"Young man, what do they call you?"

"Depends who it is doing the calling, sir; my father here, and my mother call me Jed, Jed Tanner. Others sometimes may call me You Little Bastard when I trick them. Yet others who know me well call me Twinkle on account of the quickness of my—"

"Jed, enough. Don't be over-familiar with the gentleman." Jed started to tell the reason for the name he had earned in the streets of Spitalfields. He was proud of the esteem of his name, Twinkle. The speed and deception of his dip, when his nimble hands reconnoitred the pockets of the rich and how he melted away with good pickings, had earned him the name.

"Sir," Adam intervened, "We have come many miles looking for work here. Our situation is desperate. My family is threatened with eviction. If we don't earn sufficient money for our rent, we will be separated in the workhouse."

Buckingham took sympathy on the pair.

"I see you come equipped for work," he pointed to the spade hung on Adam's back.

"That I have. We are willing and able."

"How old is the lad?" the chief engineer, William Jessop, directed the question to Adam.

"He is fifteen, sir," lied Adam. "He is small for his age. The work here will strengthen his body, no doubt."

The lordly oversight did nothing to mitigate the drudging labour of the Cutting as it progressed. From Uxbridge, a flight of forty-four locks had to be dug to lift the Cut two hundred and ninety feet to Tring Summit. Every Saturday, whatever the weather, Jed took some of his father's hard-earned money to his mother in Sclater Street. They kept their lodging and were able to rent another room. And then, a situation occurred that was unforeseen.

Adam Tanner was a conscientious worker, and his efforts drew the attention of Buckingham, who was considerate to his employees at the Cutting and on his estate. As a result, Adam was promoted to gang leader.

One of the navvies, a large, coarse fellow who always caused dissatisfaction, accused Adam of toadyism. So there was unrest one particular day, and this man, Bill Rourke, Rourkey, the gang called him, challenged Adam's authority as the gang leader.

"Hey, you, Tanner," the man shouted from the opposite side of the Cut.

Adam stood upright to see what the man wanted.

"I said, hey, you."

Someone tittered, which was when Adam realised the

shout from the other side of the Cut was a challenge. He ignored the strident voice and continued slicing through an elder root.

"Did you not hear me?" came the voice again. The man lumbered down the embankment, crossed the puddled clay to where Adam was digging and kicked the spade.

Jed was standing nearby. What he saw would remain in his memory as long as he lived. His father, who had cradled and cosseted him lovingly on his knee, turned into an entirely different man. Adam picked up the spade. Then laid the tool to one side and faced Rourkey, who grinned and loped about in front of Adam like one of the monkeys of the African continent. Staccato laughter and obscene comments in various accents echoed across the arena.

Adam's ploy in combat was to wait for the first move by his opponent. His hands were by his side. To all looking on, he looked unprepared.

Rourk swung a cumbersome right, which Adam stepped away from. He circled the opponent and waited for the next move. Another lumbering right. Adam deflected it with his left wrist. A look of surprise flicked across Rourkey's face, and then he concentrated on the next swing.

Usually, it worked. Considering Rourkey's bulk, the men he challenged would either put their fists down and concede that he was the victor, or they would back away. Adam Tanner did neither. He just smiled and stood there. And then he indicated with his left for Rourkey to have another go, which he did. And Adam feinted with a deliberately missed left and then drove home a pile-driver right to Rourkey's chin, which put him on the ground.

All around, there was silence. Rourke bullied his way

along the Cut from the first spadeful, and now he was on the ground. After it was over, Jed ran to his father. "Teach me to fight like that, dad, will you, please?" he implored.

Standing on the top of the Cut spoil heap, unseen by the men looking on, was the Marquis of Buckingham and William Jessop, the chief engineer.

"We will have to keep our eyes on yonder Mister Tanner, said Jessop. "We cannot have that behaviour going on."

"You must think it through, Jessop. Rourke has dominated the labourers since day one. Most men are afraid of him. It is time he was laid low. I'll tell you what. Tanner can fight. His movements remind me of a fellow I saw in the ring at Bermondsey last year."

Bill Rourke had been cock-of-the-roost until he came to lying in the clay, trying to focus on the men crowding around him. He nurtured a growing hatred for Adam Tanner, who had performed the unforgivable act of flooring him before all the men. Not that Tanner gloated. With his fights in the ring when the job was done, he and those he fought bore no ill will toward each other. He offered the hand of friendship to Rourke, and it was ignored.

Jed Tanner visited home each Sunday after his father received his pay at the end of the Saturday shift. Adam made a journey home once a month and was impressed by how Ruth managed their home affairs.

One Sunday, when Adam arrived, his wife was full of excitement. She revealed to him that she had saved money from their earnings and had rented a room near home, where she had begun to take in laundry. She employed four girls for scrubbing, and having installed a boiler supplying heat to some pipes, she could dry the clothes, which two more girls flat-ironed. Adam held Ruth tight and praised her to heaven for her industry.

* * *

The flight of locks toward Tring Summit was progressing slowly. It was back-breaking work, undertaken in all weather. However, Adam and Jed got used to the conditions. The pay was good, and the navigators, the navvies, were the toughest of the tough. They were competitive and thought they had done a fair day's work if they shifted twenty tons. Father and son earned their money. They worked in mud and sometimes slept in the shelter of a ditch or a tree's leeward side.

And then came the highlight of the year when the coffer dam holding back the waters of the Thames was lifted. Flags, bunting, and a military band playing for the crowd made the event colourful. There were gasps from the crowd when a new-fangled steam crane hooted loudly. With black smoke from its chimney, the wheezing and chugging crane lifted a massive plate of iron out of the water from the coffer dam.

There was a great cheer as Old Father Thames surged through Thames Lock. Sluices were opened, and the water rushed onward to merge with the River Brent.

Chapter 11

1798

The Incident at Marsworth Lock

Marsworth Lock, number 43, was the sixth in the flight leading to Tring Summit. Adam Tanner and his gang finished digging for the day. Once a week, on a Friday at the end of work, he bought beer for his men. They respected him for it and looked up to him, for in the tight-knit community of men digging the Cut, there were not any comforts. They were out in all weathers, so companionship and an easy hour after a week's heavy labour was appreciated.

Jed arrived with the newly brewed beer. He passed the bottles around, and the gang rested on the ground. They discussed the next day's work, marked out with wooden stakes by the Chainman.

Adam's gang was unique. They possessed the energy to give a fair day's work and the initiative and skill to read the land ahead. Because of this, Chief Engineer Jessop often chose them to pioneer the route where it was likely to cross challenging terrain.

He had given them the name *'Denham Deep Gang'* after they had worked an awkward stretch where the deep lock at Denham had to be dug. Adam Tanner arranged for puddling clay four feet thick rather than the usual three feet due to a persistent water spring.

To accomplish the puddling, he called for the help of a local farmer and his cows to batten down the clay. Adam's gang became an example for newly set-on labour. "If you work like the Denham Deep Gang, you won't go wrong," exclaimed Chief Engineer Jessop.

This created jealousy amongst the navvies close to Bill Rourke. Not that he had any recognised authority, but he possessed an exaggerated sense of his importance and sufficient bulk to frighten those near him into obedience. After being knocked to the ground in front of all the men, he also retained a hatred of Adam Tanner.

Rourke's revenge took a long while to plan. He wanted it to be complete, a reversal of the mud and bruising. One day, after dark, a deal was done in The Two Boats, a newly built inn at the side of the Cut. It was an expensive deal, all of one guinea. After receiving the gold, the trader handed the purchase under the table, and Rourke felt invincible.

Along with the purchase came some teaching. The pair went into a field half a mile from the Two Boats, and an hour was spent demonstrating and practising.

* * *

It was a fine Friday evening. The Denham Deep Gang had finished work for the day on Marsworth Lock number 43. Jed had gone with empty bottles to fill with beer. The men were in a relaxed frame of mind, thinking of their pay the following evening. Adam felt light-hearted. The work of his gang satisfied him, and he would be seeing Ruth on the coming Sunday.

The following day would be a challenge. Jessop warned them that the higher they rose toward Tring summit, the more consolidated the strata. In places, chalk rock was close to the surface, and they would have to resort to gunpowder to force their way onward and upward.

Jed arrived back and passed the bottles around. His turns with the spade had worked well. He was growing tall, and his lithe body was developing muscles similar to Adam's. After work, if they had privacy, they sparred together.

"You need to circle your opponent more often, Jed," said his father. "Remember, if you can tire him whilst remaining fresh, you will have him beaten in the end." Adam still disappeared some Saturday evenings to spend time in the ring, and he took delight in his son's interest in the sport.

* * *

Ruth Tanner had her eyes on a patch of land where a derelict stone building, reputedly from the fourteenth century, had been torn down. Ruth bought the derelict property from her savings. She got it at auction for a low price. What she had in mind for the land was to eventually build a smallholding in the heart of Spitalfields on which she could grow fresh produce and house cows and sheep.

Fruit and vegetables were often sold in the markets when they were partly rotten. Ruth knew that when her proposed plot came into production, she could set up a market stall and guarantee good sales by the freshness of her produce. So on their Sundays at home, Adam and Jed dug the land ready for sowing seed in the coming season.

The day after digging the soil in Spitalfields, Jed and Adam Tanner were called to the chief engineer's office. Marquis Buckingham was there, and he asked how they were fairing. "You and the boy are being treated well, Tanner, are you not?" Adam was puzzled by why they were being interviewed.

Adam was honest, saying there were times when the work was hard, "But it pays well, sir, and with the Cut, we are involved with a project that will make a great difference to this country's industry."

Buckingham nodded. "Alright, you may go. Thank you." Adam was unaware that the Marquis had seen how he had dealt with Rourke. After the fight, he offered the hand of friendship to the man. Buckingham made inquiries after the event and realised that in his employ was the fearless Dick Hammer, who he admired and respected, and the Hammer had his son with him.

* * *

Rourke was disturbed by the way Adam Tanner had fought. Tanner's awareness was uncanny, so Rourke decided on long-range revenge to keep out of the way of Tanner's fists. Bill Rourke was unused to the sophistication of a pistol, and the practice session with the man who sold it to him did not cover all contingencies.

Rourke's festering hatred made him reason that if he were to use a double charge of powder, it would ensure Tanner would die. So he poured the powder in and rammed home the ball. The lead ball was tight, so Rourke picked up a stone and hit the end of the ramrod to force the ball in. He poured gunpowder into the flash pan, cocked the weapon, and waited behind a rock on a hill at the side of the Cut.

Jed Tanner came along the Cut with bottles and passed them to the Denham Deep Gang. His father looked relaxed, leaning against the side of the Cut, which was when Rourke stood up to finish his task.

Jed's gaze drifted to the side of an outcrop of rock, some fifty feet up in the direction of the setting sun, where he had seen a movement. Then he caught a reflection, indistinct at first but then bright and sharply focussed.

"Dad," the lad warned quietly. He pointed. Adam's reflexes were quick. On Saturday evenings, he needed speed to avoid the blows. He saw the threat and leapt aside.

Rourke squeezed the trigger, but he had created a bomb out of his pistol. The spark from the flint ignited the powder. There was an explosion, and the gun blew apart, and the breech burst through Rourke's forehead.

Chapter 12

1803

The Blisworth Tunnel and Stowe

For the Denham Deep Gang, the Blisworth tunnel, north of the village of Stoke Bruerne, proved difficult due to quicksand and navigation problems. As a temporary measure, until the tunnel was complete, the construction of a horse-drawn tramway enabled transporting goods to the next stretch of the Canal.

During the Blisworth Tunnel dig, Adam left the Cutting to help Ruth with her laundry business and the smallholding, which were both doing well. The times of hardship were over. They owned their new home, still on Sclater Street, and they took in lodgers.

Jed Tanner had become the leader of the Denham Deep Gang in his father's place. He kept his father's tradition of relaxing with his gang on a Friday night. Relaxation included beer brought to the Cut by the youngest labourer if there was an alehouse near the Cutting.

As the Grand Junction Canal neared completion, Jed began considering other employment. He remembered when Buckingham called him and his father into the hut and asked how they were fairing. The Marquis must have had a good reason to invite them. Maybe, back then, he had their best interests at heart.

Usually, after midday every other Tuesday, the investors in the Cutting visited to check on progress. Jed asked Seth Lewis, the youngest in the gang, to work close to the site office, which was moved as the dig progressed, and to let him know when Buckingham came to the office.

Some three weeks later, the breathless youth came to Jed to say the Marquis had arrived. Jed dropped his spade, asked the young man to guard it, and set off to where the investors met. With some trepidation, Jed knocked on the door. Then, without waiting for a summons to enter, he thrust open the door and went in.

"What the hell is this, sir?" Jessop exploded. For the second time in Jed Tanner's experience in the site hut, a man in the shadows at the back of the room interrupted Jessop.

"Mister Jessop let the man alone; I want a few words with him. Jed, we will take a walk and discuss what you have in mind."

* * *

"Thank you for giving me some time, sir," Jed said when they were away from the hut.

"That is alright, Jed. Jessop is a good engineer, but sometimes he is short of temper." They had walked along the Cut when Buckingham stopped and faced the water. "The sooner the Blisworth Tunnel is completed, the better it will be," he said. "Transporting goods over land to connect the two completed sections of the Grand Junction slows things down far too much."

"We are two-thirds of the way through the tunnel now. However, it is difficult to work due to the possibility of subsidence."

"Yes, and thought has to be given to the safety of you people." Buckingham's mind returned to when fourteen navvies were killed when the cut through the hill collapsed. He shook away the thought.

"The Cut is progressing well, thanks to men of your courage and calibre. I will always regret that men have died in making this canal and others have sustained serious injury." The Marquis grew silent. Then, "I admired your pluck all those years ago when you came as a boy. You came into an adult situation, and your father lied to enable you to stay—"

"But—"

The Marquis held up his hand for silence. He was bringing up the past, and Jed wondered if it was a prelude to being sacked.

"I was much like you when I was young. I had a free spirit and was a rogue, a rebel. But I was not a dipper. Have you left those things behind, eh?"

Jed said nothing, only nodded, but saw the other man was smiling, "I envied you."

"Did you, sir, in what way?"

"I envied your freedom. You see, my upbringing was very restricted."

"But we were poor, weeks away from the workhouse. You envied that?"

"You could roam the streets without boots if you wanted to. You had your boots around your neck when you came."

"I preferred to walk without boots. If I stole some, they were uncomfortable. Also, they would only last until they wore out."

"You could do better than your work as a Navvy, Jed. You have resilience and inner strength. I have seen your leadership of the Denham Deep Gang as you worked the Tring Gap. The men respect you. I think you could go far."

"I do have dreams of far-off lands. I used to watch the ships and climb the rigging at Rotherhithe when the smell of spice was in the air. I saw all manner of strange goods on the dockside."

"You could come and work for me at Stowe."

"Could I, sir?"

"Yes. Listen to me. Napoleon is dominating Europe, and the war is indecisive. The press gangs are about; some of my men have been forced into naval service, and some have volunteered. I need trustworthy, hard-working men to replace them. There is much work around the estate, and you could receive training. What say you?"

"Yes, sir. I say three times yes. I want to work at Stowe."

Chapter 13

1803 - 1804

Seth Lewis

Seth Lewis was proud of his recent acquisition. To his mind, the spade was as bright and shining as the day it was made. When the leader of the Denham Deep Gang, Jed Tanner, gave it to him, he polished it with a piece of soft white rock from the cut. Tanner had given him the spade as a gesture of goodwill and friendship.

"Take care of it, Seth. May it bring you the good fortune it has given me and mine," Tanner said before he walked down the Cut to a waiting carriage.

* * *

Seth Lewis grew quickly from youth to manhood. He had experienced how the canal cutting had been a two-edged sword for communities nearby. The Cutting had disrupted a calm life that had been present for generations. Some people resented the intrusion, while others were encouraged by it. The influx of workers invigorated the communities the Cut passed through. Navvies needed food and drink, and the men in charge wanted board and lodging. Along the route of the Grand Junction Canal, the more astute local people who owned a house with extra rooms rented them out. Hannah Dean's parents were amongst those who enjoyed this good fortune.

Hannah was with her parents in The Carpenters Arms in Stoke Bruerne. She noticed a man, who looked to be in his early twenties, come through the door. His face had a homely look of warmth and sun-tanned handsomeness, which attracted her. He looked like a Navvy because of his unkempt and muddy appearance. Navvies often carried all their belongings, as the newcomer did, while away from the Cut.

Seth Lewis saw the young woman glance in his direction and felt self-conscious. His belongings were in a cloth bundle slung over his shoulder. He carried his spade wherever he went because theft amongst the canal workers was rife. The young woman was the most beautiful woman he had ever seen. He wished he had no bundle of belongings or spade with him and was in clean clothes.

Seth asked the bearded man serving ale if he had rooms to let at the inn. The man grinned and said that there was room in the stable and that he could put his spade and bundle in the manger. Laughter came from those who heard the comment.

Hannah heard what the landlord said and reacted. She saw people's reactions to what he said and did not like it. Leaping to her feet, she sprang to Seth's defence, which startled those around her, and silenced the laughter. She strode to the bar. "You should be ashamed of yourself, Mister Wainwright. A man asks a civil question, and you reply with blasphemy. You can keep your ale and your selfish hospitality. May it rot the foundations of your alehouse."

Hannah took hold of Seth Lewis' arm and pulled him to the inn door as he protested, saying he would hit the man. "I know you want to hit him, but that will achieve nothing."

Outside, the air was fresh and pure, with the smell of smoke and ale remaining inside the inn.

"I hate some of those people," she said.

Seth had been used to a masculine reaction when problems or arguments arose. Now, this beauty challenged that male edifice.

"I know you want to help me, but all I asked the publican for is lodgings."

"Is that so, mister . . . mister—?"

"Lewis."

"Mister Lewis, have you anything to say about the rudeness of the folk inside that place?"

"You haven't given me a chance to say anything, miss—"

"Dean, Hannah Dean. Will you wait here, Mister Lewis? I shall be back in three minutes, no more." With that, the young woman went back into The Carpenters Arms. As she opened the door, Seth heard the conversation quieten down, apart from a loud, "Aye-aye, she's back," Then the door slammed shut, helped by a backward kick by the dainty foot of Miss Dean.

Hannah soon came out of the door, followed by two older people.

"Mister Lewis, meet my parents, Walter and Clara Dean. They run a board and lodging residence. You can have a room there if you wish."

Hannah lay awake until the early hours of morning. She fancied she heard a blackbird piping in the dawn, and then she awoke when the sun shone full on her face through the window with open curtains. Seth Lewis had filled the short hours of her sleep. His voice echoed through dreamland and took her to the strangest of places.

* * *

Seth was amazed at his turn of good fortune. As he undid his parcel of belongings and arranged them on a side table in his room, he was vibrant with the excitement of the evening. He leant Jed Tanner's spade against a wall. During some of the few leisure hours they used to have at the Cut, Jed had taught him the rudiments of boxing. Seth could hold his own if need be, and he had been ready to go back into The Carpenters Arms to clout some heads, but the young woman stopped that.

He pictured her again. It was uncanny how her image kept returning. Seth saw her standing before him, telling him her name, Hannah Dean. In his mind, he kept saying Hannah Dean, Hannah Dean. Moreover, he pictured the fearless young woman striding resolutely back into the inn to speak to her parents, who probably felt thankful for the excuse to leave. The result was that he had lodgings.

At the breakfast table, Seth recounted what it had been like digging the canal. The picture he conveyed was that the Cutting was no place for a civilised man. "Some of us shifted twenty tons of spoil a day," he said, "Although I never quite achieved that."

"I am amazed at what you have all accomplished," Hannah said.

He nodded. "Soon, boats will ply between the Pool of London and Birmingham. It is a great achievement."

Although Seth wore a change of clothes to look respectable and made sure he had scraped mud from beneath his nails, Hannah's father had a look of distaste on his face. His wife, who he had browbeaten into submission, followed his attitude.

They disliked most of their guests and how their daughter looked at Seth. They had never seen that look, a lively interest in a person of the opposite sex.

Walter and Clara Dean had conversed at length about the future, how they would invest in a larger property and take in more guests. Hannah, away from their presence, featured in the conversations. She would work in the scullery, clean the rooms and change the linen. Washing would be a necessary task.

Now they saw their daughter growing to be a wayward girl who had a surge of independence that did not feature in the way of boarding houses. How she looked at Mister Lewis was unhealthy. When she protected the Lewis man in the Carpenters Arms, her temper was as hard as flint. Hannah's father challenged her when they sat down to dinner.

"Why do you show so much interest in Mister Lewis?"

"What concern is it of yours to whom my interests are directed?" she asked.

"Oh Hannah, please don't be unpleasant to your father," her mother pleaded.

Hannah's loyalty was often challenged in this way. However, on this occasion, the issues were different. Hannah had an attachment to their guest that differed from anything she had experienced, and her temper exploded.

"Damn you and your expectations for me. I will choose my own way in life, and if you don't like that, you can choose another to be your daughter." She stood up quickly and pushed her chair back so violently that her mother raised her hands to her ears and asked for the Lord's help.

Hannah went from the room in a carefully measured way. She did not slam the door but closed it quietly and went up the stairs to her room. A dogleg was in the stairs, where a half landing led into bedrooms two and three, and another flight of stairs led upward to Hannah's room. On the dogleg, she met Seth.

He was a trifle distant, and Hannah asked if he was alright.

"No, I am not. I heard your parents arguing with you. Your father expects far too much of you. You have your own life, Hannah."

"And I well know it. I have had my fill of being treated as a skivvy."

"What will you do?"

"If it were not for my mother, I would leave."

"Can you speak to her privately?"

"Her first loyalty is to my father, and rightly so." Seth could see that Hannah had an understanding of her mother's position. He reached for her hands, which, he could see, were trembling with emotion, and she drew close to him. He put his arms around her, and she felt comforted.

"I love you, Hannah," he said.

Looking into his eyes, she smiled. "And I love you, Seth. I love you more than anything. Shall we go away together?"

* * *

Over the next two weeks, they made plans in secret. Where to go and what to take with them. Hannah had a friend, Myra Taylor, who, with her husband, moved to Portsmouth for work. Before she went, being aware of the volatile situation between Hannah and her father, Myra invited Hannah to stay with her, so Hannah and Seth made plans to go to Portsmouth.

"I can easily find work, Hannah. Portsmouth is a busy naval town, and there is work there aplenty."

They had enough money saved between them for the journey by coach and four to Portsmouth and the cost of food for some months. During their two weeks of planning, Seth took a day off work. Keeping the trek secret from Hannah, he walked to Saint Giles Street in Northampton, where he had heard a man from Germany was a Goldsmith.

"I want a ring," he said to the man with a hooked nose and a dark complexion.

"For what purpose is the ring?"

"Engagement and marriage."

"Usually, there are two rings," the jeweller said. "The first for engagement and the second, later, for the marriage."

"One will do. What do you have?"

"Do you have the size, sir?" Seth took a crude ring out of his pocket. He had fashioned it out of the thin copper wire he had formed around Hannah's finger. Seth had gently twisted the ends together and wriggled the wire off her finger. Then he told her the wire had forged an unbreakable bond between them.

"Ah . . . the young lady has slender fingers. She is pretty too, no doubt," the jeweller said. He lifted a curtain leading to the back of the shop and came out with a tray of gold bands. He laid it on the counter, and Seth chose one. Due to the price of the rings, he chose the one with the least amount of gold, but with what the ring meant for Seth and Hannah, it was more valuable than the Crown Jewels.

Chapter 14

1804-1805

Portsmouth

Before they left Stoke Bruerne, Hannah wrote a note to her mother. She explained her reasons for leaving, gave her mother her love and left the message on the mantle shelf above the fireplace. She would have swept out the ashes and laid the fire for lighting, but the ashes remained untouched this time.

Hannah looked at her ring as the coach swayed over some rough ground. She treasured the beautiful object and was proud of the man at her side who had given it to her while they were sitting on a park bench near the Grand Junction Canal. Seth was so different to the men who had, so far, been part of her life. She could tell he wanted to protect her rather than use her, and now she felt loved.

Hannah looked out of the open window and gazed at the scenery they passed. The staccato sound of the horses' hooves disturbed a flock of crows, which flew noisily away from the coach. "Look at the birds, Seth, see how they fly away? That is how I feel. I am free and flying." She raised her arms wide, closed her eyes and imagined flying over the treetops. Seth leant over to her, held his arms wide, and clasped her hands.

"I am flying too," he said, kissing her. "If we have a daughter, she will look like you, Hannah."

And our son will look like you," she responded. "He will have a dimple in his chin, like yours," and they planned the house they would have.

"I shall use Jed Tanner's spade to dig our garden." In his mind, the spade symbolised his intent to provide for his young wife-to-be. She looked at the spade leaning against the side of the carriage. It took on a different meaning than being an implement used to till the soil.

* * *

The coach pulled into The Royal Sovereign, an inn on the street approaching the Portsmouth waterfront, and, with help, they took their trunks upstairs. Then, after a short rest, they strolled arm-in-arm toward the sea, which was shimmering in the lowering sunlight.

The gentle lapping of the water on the shingle beach was discernible as they drew near it. The sound was soothing after the cramped coach journey, and as they reached the place where there were bathing huts on the beachfront, they gazed outward at the expanse of ocean.

Myra Taylor was less than welcoming when she opened the door of her house on High Street to Hannah and Seth. Her promise of help to Hannah before she left Stoke Bruerne for Portsmouth had been made when life was going well, but now life was complicated.

"You may come in for a while." Myra looked behind her toward an open door at the far end of the short entrance hall. "But leave the trunks outside," she insisted. A drayman had transported the luggage to the door in High Street.

"What are your intentions?" Myra asked them. She seemed preoccupied, not the friendly person Hannah remembered.

"To find lodgings and work," Seth said. By the woman's attitude, he picked up that they were intruding.

"There is a lodging house in Pembroke Road. Number twenty-seven. Emma Grimmet runs it. And there is work on the dockyard or in the Navy if you are so inclined," Myra suggested.

Hannah had expected more of a welcome. She glanced around the room and detected the tired look of the furniture. It seemed things were not going well for her friend, and Hannah did not neglect what she saw. She signalled for Myra to come with her. Her friend followed Hannah to the street outside. All was quiet apart from the sound of merriment from an inn in the distance.

"What is wrong, Myra? You have changed."

"Jacob had an accident," Myra's eyes looked tearful. Hannah stepped forward. Gently held Myra's arm.

"What happened?"

"He was helping load supplies for the fleet onto a tender. The ropes gave way, and a crate fell onto his leg, which had to be amputated. Hannah, I don't know what to do."

They went back inside. Hannah sat on a sofa and asked Myra to sit by her. "Might it be that we could stay here and help you defray the costs of the house," Hannah suggested. "It would help all of us, I'm sure."

Myra looked as though she was considering the suggestion.

"Where is Jacob?" Seth asked.

"In the back room. Jacob finds meeting people hard now," Hannah remembered Jacob from when he and Myra lived in Stoke Bruerne. He was a pleasant man with a delightful sense of humour.

There was the sound of movement from behind a closed door in the wall furthest from the street. The door opened, and Jacob appeared, supporting himself on crutches. He looked weathered and worn.

"I'm sorry, Hannah, I heard the conversation. I'm unable to cope as I used to." He tapped the bandaged stump of his leg, which had been cut off above the knee.

"Oh, Jacob. Please come and sit with us. Let's talk about the good times the three of us used to have," Hannah suggested. "I'm sure Seth would like to hear about them."

Jacob nodded, shuffled to an easy chair across the room. He looked at Seth and nodded in his direction.

"You've got a good one in Hannah, Seth."

"I know," Seth told them what happened when they first met in the Carpenters Arms."

Jacob smiled. "Aye, young Hannah can be a firebrand, but she always means well with it."

Hannah smiled. "I will not tolerate injustice."

Jacob shifted in his seat. "Seth, I heard the conversation earlier, what Hannah suggested, that you stay with us and help with our cost of living. You are welcome to do that. We have spare rooms. The house tends to be narrow but goes back a fair distance from the street. Please bring in your luggage. There is also a garden attached where, when I was able, I used to grow all the vegetables we needed."

"I could help with that," said Seth.

Seth dragged in their luggage, and Myra showed them to a front bedroom on the second floor.

"Thank you so much, both of you," Jacob said, smiling for the first time since his accident.

Seth and Hannah soon became familiar with the layout of the house. It was narrow, as were most of the houses in the street. But the place was surprisingly large because of having three floors. It had a front room, a back room and a scullery through which Jacob took Seth to see the garden.

"It looks like you have apple, plum and pear trees," observed Seth.

"Yes, and I think they'll fruit well this year."

Seth bent down, stooped, and thrust his hand into the soil, which, although covered with weeds, he could see was soft and loamy. "This is good soil,"

"I mucked it each year, in Autumn-time."

"It shows," The soil was a rich, dark colour. "We will easily get this producing again," Seth recalled the harsh conditions he worked in with the Denham Deep gang during the excavation of Blisworth Tunnel.

* * *

Myra and Jacob were close friends with an Anglican vicar, loved by his flock because of his rebelliousness to some of the church's traditions. He consented to marry Seth and Hannah at short notice.

"Better to accept some of the expected formalities than live in sin," he said, with a knowing smile and a tap on the nose. "A law was passed in 1753 called the Clandestine Marriage Act. I'm afraid I have to disagree with it, as do some other clergymen. We will read the banns, this has to be done for the marriage to be valid, but we will overlook the parish requirements. You have two witnesses, Myra and Jacob, and your marriage will be recorded in the Parish Register. Hannah and Seth, you will be married in the sight of God, which is what matters. By the way, did you know God has a name?"

"Surely not; he is God, our Creator" said Hannah.

"Where did you get the idea that the Almighty has a name?" Seth asked.

"From the Bible, the Hebrew scriptures. The name is in the original Hebrew-Aramaic scriptures over seven thousand times. Do you have a Bible?"

Hannah nodded.

"Then take a look at Psalm 83 verse 18."

* * *

The marriage took place with Jacob Taylor giving away Hannah Dean. He proudly escorted Hannah down the aisle on new crutches, wearing a new tricorn hat and frock coat.

As the weeks passed, Seth tilled the soil in the garden of their lodgings. Cabbage, carrot and leek seeds were sown, and fifteen rows of potatoes would produce a bountiful crop. Seth looked at his day's work. The garden was transformed.

"Give me the spade, Seth; I'll clean it." Jacob was sitting on a bench near the door leading out of the kitchen. "Come and sit down awhile." Jacob patted the bench and held out his hand for the spade.

The next day Seth went in search of work but found nothing. So he stepped into an alehouse called The Royal Sovereign on his way home. An alehouse was often an excellent place to hear about available work, and he chatted to the landlord.

"Portsmouth is a naval place," The landlord said. "They are desperate for more men, with the French threatening to invade." The landlord was subdued and fell silent, thinking of how life in the future could change.

* * *

Seth continued to prepare the land. He needed to enrich the soil with manure, and Samuel Lynch, the landlord at The Royal Sovereign, was pleased when Seth offered to muck out the stables. Lynch suggested that Seth could do it regularly for pay, so, although small, Seth had an income. After several journeys with a wheelbarrow, he had a heap of manure in a corner of their land for feeding the crops.

It was usual during the evening for Hannah and Seth to sit near the fire in the front room with Myra and Jacob. Hannah had seen the heap of horse manure and, realising there would be too much for their garden, suggested that profit could be made if they sold it.

"Maybe profit could be made differently," said Jacob. "We could have a market stall and sell fruit and vegetables."

"You and I could run the stall," Myra suggested.

"We could. What say you, Seth, Hannah?"

"It's worth trying. Seth and I could do the work on the land." Hannah looked at Seth for confirmation.

"I'ld say we try it out."

"I will help with the land, too," said Myra.

"And I will make food and drinks for you and do weeding as best I can," said Jacob. "And I'll clean the tools. By the way, where did you get your spade? It seems special to you."

"Someone I used to work with, named Jed Tanner."

Chapter 15

1805

The Giant Walk of a Slender Man

There was raucous noise, shouting and laughter from an inn on one of the streets Seth and Hannah walked by.

"It's about Napoleon," Seth heard the name mentioned.

"By all accounts, that upstart is a great menace," Hannah said. She had sometimes heard snatches of news. In Stoke Bruerne, amongst the gangs of Navvies, there was often mention of the little corporal from Corsica who had been active on the other side of the English Channel. Over recent months the threat of invasion had risen to a high level.

"The Navy is on alert, and word is out that Admiral Nelson intends to end Napoleon," Seth said.

"I know, and some of the Stoke Bruerne men enlisted in the 58th Regiment of Foot a short while back. The village was abuzz with the threat of invasion."

Seth looked out over the ocean. Picked out in the early moonlight was the silhouette of the Isle of Wight. Low down, in the dark area between land and sea, lights shimmered on the water. Seth pointed into the distance, where he could see the lighter colour of the gun decks of the ships of the fleet. "See there, Hannah, the Ships of the Line. Out yonder lies the Victory, the Admiral's flagship."

At ten thirty on the night of September the thirteenth, Vice Admiral Horatio Nelson said farewell to Emma Hamilton at Merton, near London and travelled by Post-chaise to Portsmouth. He arrived at The George Hotel at six in the morning. He breakfasted and walked, with some of his officers, to meet the Resident Commissioner of Portsmouth Dockyard, Captain Sir Charles Saxton.

Walking to the dockyard, people recognised the slightly built Vice Admiral. Since fear was in the air about Napoleon's desire to subjugate Britain by invasion, word soon got around that Nelson was in town, ready to command the fleet and sail against the French.

After conversing with the Dockyard Commissioner, Nelson returned to The George, where he met George Rose, the President of the Board of Trade, and George Canning, the Treasurer of the Navy, who came to wish him well.

That morning, Seth Lewis was also walking the streets. He was looking for some land where he could expand the market garden. The market stall trade was lively. Portsmouth was a busy place, growing with the crowded presence of the Navy and dockside workers who came from all regions of Great Britain and further afield.

When they were eating their mid-day meal, Seth told Hannah what he had seen earlier, "I saw Nelson. He and some of his men were walking to the dockyard."

"He is a great man."

"He is a great man. He is not of great stature. He looked care-worn, but something about him made the crowd's huzzas special. He took off his hat, Hannah. Nelson waved his hat at me. I waved mine back, and he smiled. He has made the Navy better for ordinary seamen. Did you know he gets seasick at the start of his voyages?"

"That cannot be."

"It is so."

* * *

The public adored Nelson for his courage and leadership, and most people overlooked his blatant affair with Emma Hamilton. The press at times caricatured Horatio and Emma, but now . . . now, with the palpable fear of invasion stalking the streets of England, the crowds gathered to cheer him on. Now no one mocked him.

Came the time for embarkation. When Nelson heard the crowd noise growing louder on the road outside the hotel where he was staying, he requested the Landlord to let him and his party out of the back door. They went into Penny Street, then Green Row, and through a tunnel close to King's Bastion, heading to the beach near a row of bathing huts.

The Admiral was resplendent in his uniform, walking through town from his lodging with a group of officers. Thousands of people were cheering as he made his way to the launch, standing by to take him to his ship.

Seth and Hannah joined the crowd who gathered to see the fleet set sail. As the Victory's sails began to fill and the fleet slowly moved away from its mooring, the crowd's cheering grew louder still. "Godspeed to Nelson on his voyage." Oh, how they cheered their hero, Rear Admiral Horatio Lord Nelson of the Nile, Duke of Bronté, on his way to meet the French.

When Nelson walked by, Seth and Hannah were standing at the front of the crowd. What they heard him say stayed with them for their long years together.

"I had their huzzahs before; I have their hearts now."

Chapter 16

1805-1806

Oh, How the Years Are Marked

And marked by what events and by whom? If only we could foresee events and make wise decisions. Having heard of the death of Nelson, Seth and Hannah and their friends Myra and Jacob were having some quiet time together. The town of Portsmouth was subdued, as was the nation when the news of Nelson's death was received.

"There will be no invasion, so something good was achieved," said Jacob.

"And we can look ahead to better times," Hannah had in mind that the work they had accomplished with their smallholding would not be ruined by the French. Small beginnings, but at least the four living on High Street had sufficient income to keep their home.

The Market started early the next day. Traders began setting up their stalls at six in the morning, so Hannah and Seth retired that night at ten o'clock.

An hour later, Myra Taylor put some washing on a clothes-horse near the fire to dry overnight. She blew out the candles. It seemed to be a peaceful night. There was a full moon when she glanced out of the window. It was lighting the garden, and the stars were shining brilliantly. Myra lingered there for a while, captivated by the starry heavens, and then she retired upstairs to bed and got close to Jacob. They held each other tight and drifted off to sleep.

They were woken up by violent knocking on their door. The light was shining through the curtains. *The moon is silver, not orange,* she thought, her mind confused by sleep, and there was noise, a crackling noise, and a smell of smoke. She coughed. The door was hit hard again, and Seth barged in, followed by Hannah.

"Out. Out quickly. The house is ablaze. Get clothes," Seth shouted. Myra, now fully awake, leapt out of bed and drew the curtains. Fortunately for the moonlight, she could see her way to the wardrobe. Hannah, who had a candle lighting the way, grabbed a robe from a hook on the door, dashed to Myra, covered her and helped her get clothes from the wardrobe for her and Jacob.

"Come with me," Hannah held Myra's arm, and they ran to the back bedroom with the clothes, and Hannah threw them out of the window.

Seth helped Jacob, half-carrying him along the landing to the back bedroom where Hannah and Myra were calling to people below. "Jump," one of them shouted up.

"We are using sheets to help us get down," Hannah shouted.

There was the sound of breaking glass and shouting at the front of the house. Seth dragged the sheets off his and Hannah's bed.

"Hold this sheet, Hannah; let me have the end." He stood by the open window, tied another sheet to the first one, found the other end and made it into a small loop, enough for a foot to fit into.

"You first, Jacob; put your foot in the loop." The others lifted him to the window. He wriggled out, holding onto the window sill and then the sheet. Seth took the strain and lowered Jacob to the group of men and women below.

"Come on, you'll be alright, Jake, quickly now," said one of the neighbours, Henry Dalton, a big, burly fellow who held Jacob steady and released his foot from the sheet.

"Alright, he's down. Take up the sheet," Dalton shouted. There was an explosive sound from the front of the house, a roaring and an odd cyclic noise and hissing.

"Now you, Hannah." Seth held the loop in the sheet for her to put her foot in.

"No, Myra first." Seth looked at Hannah. In the height of danger, they kissed.

"Get your foot in, Myra." Hannah helped her scramble onto the windowsill. Seth once again took the strain and lowered Myra to the ground. And then it was Hannah's turn.

"What about you, Seth?" Hannah held the sheet, the loop ready to step into.

"We will tie another sheet," he grabbed one off his and Hannah's bed, and they quickly tied them. "When you are safely down, I will tie it to the headboard. Quickly now."

"I love you, Seth. With all my heart, I love you."

"And I love you." Then, a crashing noise occurred, and flames appeared at the bedroom door.

"The roof is giving way. Be quick, you people," shouted Dalton. Seth lifted Hannah to the window. She sobbed and kissed him, and he lowered her down.

"She's free," shouted Dalton. Seth pulled up the sheets and looked behind him. The room was lit as the flames took hold. He glanced at the bedposts, rushed with the sheet to the footboard, and tied it onto a post. He could feel the fierce heat of the fire as he pulled the bed near the window and threw out the sheets.

He looked below at the group of people, saw the woman he loved, and glanced at the ceiling above, which began to catch fire. There was a loud creaking noise as the timbers started to give way. Strange, at these times, what thoughts come to mind? As he went hand over hand down the sheets, Seth Lewis thought of Admiral Nelson in his desperate time of need. When he lay dying after being mortally wounded by a French marksman from the mizzen-top of the Redoutable, Nelson asked the Captain of the Victory, "Well, Hardy, how goes the battle? How goes the day with us?" And Hardy replied, "Very well, My Lord."

Seth's feet touched the ground just as the roof at the rear of the house gave way. They all rushed away from the flames and the falling debris. From the safety of the large garden that helped them earn a modest income, they watched as their house was consumed by fire.

Chapter 17

1805 - 1810

Marked For Survival

"We have lost almost everything," Myra said, looking at the clothes rescued from their wardrobe. Her thoughts went back to the washing she left to dry. A spark from one of the logs must have flown onto the washing and set it on fire. Myra was silent, wondering how to tell the others. She looked at Jacob, sitting on the ground. Their burning home reflected in his eyes. He struggled to get up. She helped him. "Even my crutches have gone, Myra."

Seth looked at the remains of the building. The houses nearby seemed unaffected by the fire. He went to Jacob, leant down and offered his hands. "Hold on to me, Jake, until we know what to do." Jacob clutched Seth's hands. Hannah noticed Seth's spade a few yards away. He had left it in the ground when he finished digging earlier. They had been planning a spring successional sowing that afternoon.

Hannah was barefoot and was wearing only thin nightclothes, but she walked over the bare earth, grasped the spade and took it to Jacob. "Here is a makeshift crutch. It may be heavier than your other crutches, but it will suffice." She offered it to him, handle first.

Holding on to Seth with his left hand, Jacob took the spade from Hannah. He placed the tip of the spade on the ground and let go of Seth's hand. He moved the spade forward, put his weight on it and gently walked ahead. The steel of the spade rang on the granite cobbles.

"We will hear you coming with that," said Henry Dalton. "But never mind, it'll help you for now." People fighting the fire at the front of the building came to the back through the burned-down side gate.

"Thank goodness you are safe," said a tall man, Arthur Price, leading the others, both men and women. In the light of the fire and the moonlight, they looked dishevelled, smudged with soot, and soaked with water.

"We did our best," Price said. "There was insufficient water. The well is fifty paces down the road. The men with the pump were not here soon enough to quench the fire."

"We thank you all for what you tried to do," said Hannah. She grew silent.

Seth grasped her and held her close. "Thank God we all survived. We have each other. *Things* don't matter," he said, offering a silent prayer that they had all survived.

"What shall we do now?" Jacob shouted to no one in particular. Those gathered around felt the enormity of the situation. A man who lived nearby on Britain Street came from the back of the group. He had a strong French accent when he spoke, saying his name was Marcel Dumanoir.

"I am sorry. We were too late with our fire pump to save your house." The man sounded dejected. "But I have somewhere you can stay," he said. "Have you saved any of your belongings?"

"Our clothes and this," Jacob said, one hand holding Seth's arm and the other holding the spade aloft. He held it high as if as a challenge. He had got his fighting spirit back. Jacob was a fighter, not literally, unless there was a need. But until Hannah and Seth arrived, his amputation made him lose the will to fight against the odds. Before the accident, he had been a lively, self-sufficient man. Jacob now had Myra, his friends, a few clothes, an improvised crutch, and no house. But he had heard Seth's words to Hannah that they had survived the fire and still had each other. The event re-energised his fighting spirit. He turned with anger and faced the fire.

"As God is my witness," he said, loudly as if addressing the fire, with the spade held high. "I swear that this will not be the end of us. It is a beginning. Thank you, sir," he said to Dumanoir. "We will accept your offer for a short while if we may, and we will be forever in your debt."

The crowd gradually left, all with aching limbs and sad faces. Monsieur Dumanoir led the way to his house on Britain Street. It was in the Georgian style, and the entrance was through a wide gate between pillars of Portland Stone.

As they reached the door, a servant, waiting for Dumanoir to arrive, opened it. He helped the older man off with his coat and hung it on a coat rack.

"Louis will shortly show you to some rooms where you can stay. Oh, I do not know your names, Mister . . ." Dumanoir looked at Jacob.

"Taylor, I am Jacob Taylor. This is Myra, my wife, and our two friends here are Hannah and Seth Lewis."

Dumanoir asked the servant, "Louis, bring Mister Taylor my father's crutches, will you?" Dumanoir approached Jacob. "You will be best with proper crutches. You may use those that belonged to my late father. Please, all of you, sit awhile and try to relax. By the way, my men are bringing the clothes you managed to save." Dumanoir indicated where to sit and went to a sideboard, on which there was wine and spirits. He took glasses from a cupboard. "What is your fancy?" he asked. "We have a

Cognac, a particularly old one, Rum, direct from Jamaica, and a wine selection. There is a tawny wine that I enjoy. Considering your distressing situation, I would recommend this wine. It is rich and easy on the palate. It is from the Pedro Domeque winery and, believe it or not, it is called Nelson." He saw surprised looks. "Yes, my wife and I narrowly escaped Madame la Guillotine. She was after our blood. I am the Comte de la Foret Saint-Sever, and I am eternally grateful to your Admiral Nelson for defeating the Navy of Bonaparte. Please, let me help you, as your country has helped me. Please drink." He poured and handed over the generously filled glasses.

A woman came into the room, and Dumanoir introduced her as Sophie, his wife. She looked concerned. It was she who, upon looking from her window and seeing the fire, called her husband.

"Please be confortable in this 'ouse," her English was not as good as her husband's, but her looks and intentions were most sincere.

A clock struck two in a nearby room. The servant, Louis, returned with the crutches. Louis was a tall man whose skin was like rich ebony. His features were African.

Monsieur Dumanoir addressed his guests. "Tidy yourselves up and try to have a good night's rest. I will see you downstairs for breakfast on the morrow. Sleep well. Please show our friends to the bedrooms, will you, Louis?"

The servant led the way upstairs, and they reached a landing. "Please follow me," said Louis, who spoke English well but had a distinctive French accent. Hannah caught up with him.

"Thank you for helping us," she said.

"That is my pleasure, Madame. But it is Le Comte de la Foret Saint-Sever who helps."

"Where are you from?" Hannah asked. "She was curious. She had never seen a person like him before. His colour and his features looked distinctive, even regal.

"I am from the Kingdom of the Soussais. I was an enslaved person and brought to France. Le Comte does not believe slavery is how people should be treated, so he freed me. However, I have chosen to stay as his helper."

"The Count is a very thoughtful man."

"He is. He treats his workers well. He is an inventor and has a factory near the dockyard."

"What does he make in his factory?"

"He is a maker of fire pumps, le pompe à incendie. He and some of his men attended the fire at your house, but they heard about it too late, and he could not stop the burning. But please, here are your rooms. Hot water is in the bathtubs, and towels are on stands."

Chapter 18

1810-1812

A Change in Fortune

It was morning. A faint light was showing through the curtains. Hannah looked at the Ormolu and marble clock on the mantle shelf above an ornate fireplace. There was a beautifully lifelike, although gold-coloured figurine of a winged angel sitting gracefully to the left of the hour dial. Seth stirred and turned to face her, leant across the large bed and kissed her shoulder.

Despite the night-time tragedy, Hannah, through exhaustion, had slept well. The help given by Marcel Dumanoir lessened the impact of the fire.

The knock on the door that had awoken her came again, louder, and a soft voice said, "Madame et Monsieur, breakfast is in one-half hour."

"Thank you . . . thank you," said Seth.

"Very well, Monsieur."

* * *

The conversation was easy that morning in the dining room. Once again, the Count apologised for not arriving soon enough to save the burning house. His demeanour was kind and sincere, not aloof, as someone might be with an aristocratic upbringing. He and his wife's approach to their guests showed that they respected and valued the company of others, regardless of their social standing.

"How did you know about the fire, sir?" asked Hannah.

"My wife, Sophie, saw it from our bedroom window. Hannah, please do not call me sir. Let me explain. I informed you about our escape from France because a French accent in your country arouses suspicion. Another thing, as far as I am concerned, we are no longer part of the aristocracy, so please call us by our first names, Marcel and Sophie."

Marcel saw Jacob studying the ornate surroundings of the room. Jacob was trying to rid his mind of the images of his burning house. The riches surrounding him brought into question the unfairness of the haves in this life and the have-nots.

"Jacob, let me explain more about our presence in your country and this house." There was a soft knock, and Louis opened a panelled door for a young woman, who entered with a serving trolley on which were silver serving dish tureens.

"Ah, thank you, Jane. Let us enjoy our food, and I will explain why we are in England."

The serving girl, Jane, took the lids off the tureens, and the smell of bacon and other choice morsels arose.

"From his boyhood, my father was a friend of the German astronomer Friedrich William Herschel. Herschel escaped to England after the French took over Hanover in 1757. Father was an inventor, and he was a brilliant engineer. With his connection to Herschel, my father applied himself to making astronomical instruments. He was a good teacher. He taught me mathematics and engineering. But then unrest began in France, so my father moved to Portsmouth. I am forever in his debt because his teaching enabled me to continue with progressive scientific work after he died.

"As an aristocratic family, we have considerable inherited wealth, which my father could transfer to

England. I try not to be selfish with that wealth." Marcel stopped talking, and, for a minute or so, they all ate. And then Sophie Dumanoir took up the explanation.

"In France, Marcel's father, Le Comte de la Foret Saint-Sever, Jacques Dumanoir, began to make the sextant for French Navy. They need them and did British Navy. After some years here in Portsmouth supplying British Navy, business was good. Well established, you say?" Sophie's gaze drifted to the window overlooking the back garden. She paused in her explanation, thinking of life in her beloved homeland, France, and how it had become unbearable.

"Marcel and me had stay in France to care for family estate. We manage to sell estate to aristocrat with courage and no sense and," Sophie indicated the furnishings and ornaments, which were tastefully arranged around the room, "We move our belongings to England. It was very secret time for us. For while, we live as commoners in 'ouse in Villedieu-les-Poêles. It was different for us. We were enjoy our lives together without obligation that control us. But revolution started, and too dangerous for us in France. We journey to Calais and then find ship to England. Calais was so dangerous."

"So you came to England, and Marcel and his father carried on making sextants," Seth summarised, not knowing in detail what a sextant was used for.

"That is correct. And then my father died. I continued with the instrument making and general engineering."

"Have you made fire pumps for long?" Hannah asked.

"I designed our pump eighteen months ago. We completed the first one three months ago. We have tested it thoroughly, and have excellent water pressure from the hose. It reaches about forty yards. It was the pump which we brought to your house fire." Sophie saw the downcast look in her husband's eyes.

"Marcel put many hours work in fire pump. It is used three times before fire at your house, and every time successful. The fires stopped."

"You need to build a tower on the highest place in Portsmouth, and it has to have a large bell to warn the town of fire and ready your men to transport the pump," said Hannah authoritatively. "You should have it drawn by horses. The pump needs to be larger than your present one, and it would be best for four horses to pull it. You need more than one pump if there is more than one fire." How to improve fighting a fire seemed simple to her.

Dumanoir stood so quickly that he startled the others and knocked over a water carafe.

"Mon Dieu, you have it, my girl. You have the answer." He grabbed the carafe before it emptied, took a serviette and mopped up the pooled water. "I must see the County Surveyor, Monsieur Vandamm, "I will return later today."

The months passed. Charles Vandamm was impressed by the Dumanoir Fire Pump, notably when he attended a demonstration. Very soon, an observation tower equipped with a warning bell was constructed on Portsdown Hill, giving a perfect view over the busy town and the docks.

A larger pump was designed and built. Pulled by four horses, the 'Dumanoir Fire Engine', built in Portsmouth, gained the interest of towns throughout Hampshire and wider afield.

Hannah Lewis was introduced to the design loft at the Dumanoir works. She had a natural aptitude for invention and leadership. Her husband, Seth, became head of the first team of eight firemen.

With the growth of the Dumanoir and Son Fire Appliance works, help was needed to run the homes on the estate. Sophie and Myra, who became her reliable companion, applied themselves to the task.

Marcel Dumanoir, the kindly Frenchman who wanted to help others, had a house built on his estate with separate quarters for Hannah, Seth, Myra and Jacob.

Jacob, with a false leg designed and made by Dumanoir, became the head gardener on the estate. He treasured the spade that Seth gave him because of the quality of its manufacture. But Jacob was frustrated when trying to buy one for his assistant gardener, Luke Freeman, to use. He could not find any information about the maker, T S, according to the stamped marks in the shank of the spade.

Chapter 19

1797-1812

Lukas Freimark

Lukas Freimark wanted to be called Luke Freeman to complete his identity change. He was twenty-eight years old, Jewish and had to leave Hamburg, the place of his birth, with some urgency. The problem started when he was thirteen. It was a simple situation that grew out of all proportion. A neighbourhood bully, Arnulf Holpp, aged fifteen, was big for his age. Holpp always picked on the boys smaller than himself because he was sure to win.

Lukas observed the performance several times and was angered by what was happening. One particular time a twelve-year-old boy, Franz Jensen, a friend of Lukas, had been picked on.

Franz was approached by boys who were intent on bullying him. At the front was Arnulf Holpp. He flexed his muscles and rained blows on Franz, leaving him bloodied on the ground.

Lukas vowed to get revenge. The preparation, mental and physical, took several years. During this time, he avoided Holpp, but when he heard of further beatings, he was left unsettled and angry for days afterwards. He practised every evening in a run-down stable near his home. During the day, he worked in the garden of Schloss Bergedorf, refining his skills as a landscape gardener, for which he had a natural ability. At the age of nineteen, Lukas became the assistant Head Gardener at Schloss Bergedorf.

It was Shabbat Eve, and Lukas was nearing the synagogue. The traditional yarmulke headwear emphatically pronounced that he was a Jew to all he passed, including Arnulf Holpp. Holpp had a deep bass voice, particularly when challenging a target.

The voice rang loud and clear across the market square. "Hey, Jew. Come here; I want you here." Lukas walked on. He slowed down as he heard heavy footsteps approaching from behind. There were many people in the market square. They all heard Holpp's voice echoing off the surrounding buildings, and they stopped, curious to see the outcome. Some of them had experienced Holpp. All victims of his taunts fearfully and quickly evaded him, often accompanied by shouts of, "Coward, run away, you coward," or more offensive words if women were present.

Lukas removed his yarmulke and put it in his pocket, steeling himself for what would come. He turned and smiled. Felt his prepared, toughened knuckles and stood still, with arms akimbo. Holpp slowed and stopped, moving his arms about as if loosening his muscles, ready to attack. Usually, with Holpp's method, his victim would have retreated, but instead, Lukas moved forward.

What Holpp didn't know was that Lukas had found a book describing travels in the land of Japan by the explorer Samuelis Vorsacht. In the book, the author recounted how he heard of and then learned a way of fighting called Empty Hand, in the town of Naha, on Okinawa Island. Vorsacht explained the technique through his writing and drawings, which, although in a simple form, were enough for Lukas to become proficient in the art.

The move was so fast that Holpp, a tall man of broad, muscular form, was hit on the chest, in the heart region, before he could defend himself. The blow followed Vorsacht's description that such an 'Empty Hand' blow should be aimed to terminate a fist's depth into the enemy's body.

When he hit Arnulf Holpp, Lukas thought of his friend, Franz, who this man had hit unmercifully for no reason back in those childhood years. And he thought too of the other victims of the bully. From around the market square came cheers and clapping.

Holpp, on the ground, was not moving. It happened that a doctor, Reinhardt Kranz, was passing. His son had been the victim of the bully. The doctor knelt on the cobbles at Holpp's side and put his fingers on the swarthy neck of the man on the ground. There was no sign of a pulse. Kranz grimaced, got close to Holpp's head, put his ear close to the man's mouth, and shook his head.

"He is dead." A gasp arose from those gathered around.

"He deserved it," said a man loudly, who had been a victim in the past. The doctor saw blood pooling on the ground, reached his hand behind Holpp's head and felt a sharp stone projecting from a joint between the cobbles. His fingers touched a hole in the dead man's skull.

"You must come with me," said the doctor. "Leave this man lying here. Come now, quickly."

Doctor Kranz had contacts in the town of Portsmouth, in England, so Lukas was quickly smuggled out of Germany and escaped execution. He had a fresh start with a changed identity. He became Luke Freeman, a landscape gardener with an English name and a German accent, assisting Jacob Taylor at the Dumanoir estate.

Chapter 20

1812 -1814

Amos Washington

Luke Freeman became head gardener at Chateau Dumanoir, as Marcel and Sophie decided to call their home. It was with sadness that they attended the funeral of Jacob Taylor, who, despite his disability, had always ensured that the large formal garden of the estate was immaculately kept.

Lukas Freimark, Luke Freeman, showed promise as a landscape architect when he assisted Jacob in designing and making a glasshouse. It was heated by a stove from which, in due season, hot water circulated through large-diameter cast iron pipes. The glasshouse was home to exotic trees grown in espalier form and to tender vegetables, salads, and flowers for the table in the colder months.

Not long after Jacob's death, Luke spoke to Marcel Dumanoir about the need for assistants.

"I can see that with the work involved, you need more than one assistant," said Marcel.

We will need three assistants with the work we discussed.

"You mean the lake and groups of oak and other native trees as a backdrop that you were suggesting. You have found that to be feasible?"

"I have examined the soil. It will be excellent for the growth of trees. But, if that is what you wish to do, we will need able men to assist in deepening the part of the estate near the stream, and we will need to channel the stream to the place suitable for it to fill the lake."

"And you will need to create an outflow to prevent the lake overfilling," said Hannah Lewis, who had entered to speak to Marcel. She was highly respected as an engineer with an eye for innovation.

Luke nodded at her. He respected Hannah's concepts. "The men will need to be retained after the digging," he said. "More maintenance will be required than there is now with a lake added to the estate."

Marcel was pacing the room. "Yes, of course. I understand what you say. Much construction work will be involved, and I want the landscaping completed as soon as possible. It will take time to become fully mature, but Sophie and I want to enjoy some of your visions of the lake and the trees. You do need more help. Hire the men."

The most helpful places to find labour were at the dockside and local taverns. Talk amongst the men frequenting the bars was often to do with work — or the lack of it. So during the week following Marcel's instruction to hire the labour, Luke Freeman spent evenings visiting the taverns but drinking little in them.

On the fourth night, whilst standing at the bar, Luke heard some deeply sunburned men at a nearby table talking to others with pale features about having just disembarked from their latest voyage. They spoke of quaint places and how interesting it had been to see trees and lands so different from those they recognised.

"But it is good to be home," acknowledged one of the sailors, a man who looked to be in his early thirties. "I will not sail again," he said.

"Why is that, Amos?" asked one of the paler men.

"Because I love England, and I have a wife."

"Then why did you go this time?" asked another.

"Because we needed money, and now the voyage is finished, I must find work," replied Amos.

Luke approached the group.

"I can offer work as a gardener," he said. Amos was startled by the voice behind him but was immediately interested. The others at the table glanced up at the stranger with a foreign accent.

"When can I begin working for you?" asked Amos.

"Tomorrow, if you wish. It will be heavy work; are you able to do that?"

"I was ship's carpenter and was involved repairing chafing gear at odd times when there was no carpentry to be done."

"You were doing that round The Horn and Good Hope too, eh Amos," stated another sunburned character. "Have you any work for me as well, sir?" he asked.

"I have, and for yet another man. I need three who are prepared to put their backs to the work. Do I have another?" The final man of those who had been in tropical climes nodded.

"You have me, sir. I am more than willing."

"We are off the Ariadne and have been laid off her. She is hove-too for re-fit and careening," explained Amos.

"Very well. You start in the morning at Chateau Dumanoir on Britain Street. On the right of the building, you will see a glass house. I will meet you there at eight of the clock."

Luke Freeman laid his landscape plan on a table in the glasshouse. The remaining wild area of the estate was ideal for what he had in mind. A stream fell underground near an outcrop of rock. It re-emerged one hundred and fifteen paces away, beyond a shallow valley ideal for an ornamental lake with a backdrop of trees.

"You could stock the lake with fish," Luke had explained to Marcel. He had tried to remember the English for Karpfen, Aal, und Brasse. "Ah, I remember now that your word for Karpfen is carp. Aal, you call eel. The other, I do not know your word for, Brasse."

* * *

There was a knock on the glasshouse door, and Luke opened it to the three sailors, suitably dressed for work.

"Hello, Amos; thank you and your friends for accepting my offer."

"It came at the right time for us," Amos pointed to his colleagues as he introduced them. "Peter Cornish and this is Gabriel Dunn."

Freeman extended his hand to each of them and asked what their work was aboard ship.

"I was a spun-yarn winch operator, making and repairing ropes," said Cornish.

"And I, too, worked upon spun yarn," added Gabriel Dunn. "That work busied us most of the time. Rigging is worn by weather and seawater. It always needs repairing or replacing,"

"You will find the work here more interesting than your work at sea. It may be just as tiring, but your working day will have regular breaks. Meals are given regularly in the room at the end of the glasshouse. Are you familiar with observing a plan such as this one?"

The men gathered around the landscape plan devised by Freeman. It was three feet by two feet, executed using pen and watercolour wash. A note describing each feature was written numerically in a column on the lower right. The appropriate numeral was written in large, Germanic-style text over the appropriate element part of the plan.

"I have seen such work in books upon travel that interests me. I was taught to read by my father," said Amos.

"You have the advantage over me, Amos. I cannot read or write," said Gabriel.

"And neither can I write," admitted Cornish, "Other than signing my name with a cross."

"Then I may be able to help with that," said Freeman. "If you so wish, I can teach you to read and write in winter when we have long dark evening hours." Freeman tapped the figure one in a list on the corner of his plan. "Do you see this mark? That is figure one. Remember the shape of the number and the sound of how you say it. One. Do you see where figure one is placed on the drawing? The area is coloured blue, representing the large ornamental lake that you men and I are to construct."

Amos Washington noticed Luke's accent again, that sometimes when he spoke the letter 'w', it sounded like 'v'. "We will begin the lake area tomorrow," said Luke. "There are documents which you must sign or add your mark. They state your pay rate and work hours. By signing the document, you agree to the conditions. Please, go to the room at the end of the glass-house. There is a table and chairs. Please be seated and think of questions you want to ask me. I will join you shortly."

Two men, Dunn and Cornish, made their way to the room, but Amos hung back. He was curious and looked Luke Freeman in the eye. "Sir, you have a foreign accent and an English name," he said. Freeman smiled.

"Yes, I am sure you find that unusual. I will explain sometime, but not now."

The room they sat in was comfortably laid out. It was equipped with a hearth and a sink. And a wide cast-iron stove, with a door enclosing a lit fire, had a steaming kettle on it. Three documents, a quill for the signing, an ink well, and a sheet of blotting paper lay on the table.

"Amos, as you can read, please read this document and discuss its content with your colleagues," Luke requested. "It states what I told you earlier, the pay rate and the hours to be worked. Then, please sign or put your mark in this position if you agree with what it says." Luke pointed to the place for the signature or mark and then went to the door leading to the formal garden. "I will give you time to discuss the work you are being offered. Then, if you have any questions, please ask."

The three new workers signed the documents without asking questions, and work commenced the next day. After three weeks of excavating the area designated for the lake, it became apparent more labour was needed. Luke asked Amos, with whom he had developed a friendship if he knew other men suitable for the work.

More labour was set on from the berthed Ariadne. Work went on apace, and then, some two months after the commencement of work, the lake area was dug, and the stream was channelled into the excavation. Finally, the surrounding area, including the small, elongated hill created from spoil excavated from the lake area, was planted with oak, elm, silver birch and hazel.

The men sat on a grassy area overlooking their work and rested. It was accompanied by large measures of middling ale, porter and a toast to thank them for their massive effort by an ebullient Marcel Dumanoir, his wife and their twenty-year-old son, Matthew.

Matthew separated from the crowd and strolled around the newly planted woodland toward a deeply tanned man planting a young tree he had taken off a cart.

"What tree is that?" asked the young man.

"It is an oak tree, sir," said Amos as he heeled in the sapling. He watered it.

"How long will it take to grow?"

"See that tree yonder, in the hedgerow on the horizon?" Amos pointed to the stately form. "That is an English oak. Judging by its girth, it must be five hundred years old at least."

"Will I see the tree you planted reach its maturity?"

"Maybe your great-grandchildren will, young sir. Would it not be good to live forever and see the work of our hands in these last months grow to be a mature scene of great beauty?"

"It would indeed be good."

Amos straightened up to ease his back, rubbed it and leant on his spade.

"May I put some trees in?" Mathew asked.

"You can indeed. There is a variety of young trees here. Which would you like to plant?" Amos pointed to the different varieties and named them.

"I want to plant oak. I have heard that the ships of the line are built of English oak."

"They are. Did you know that it took over two-thousand oak trees to build Admiral Nelson's ship, the Victory?"

"Really? All of our new woodland to build one ship."

"Yes. A costly undertaking for our forests. Here, use this spade quickly and plant more oak. It might be needed for more Ships of the Line." He laughed, and so did Matthew.

The lad planted ten oak trees, following Amos' direction to heel them in. The sun glinted brilliantly on the blade of the spade. "This is a nice tool, sir," said Matthew. As he lifted the spade to examine it, the blade touched a stone, and the high-carbon steel rang with a tone as clear as a bell.

Chapter 21

1815-1820

The Swift Passage of Years, an Intermission

Years and events passed by like dust over a windswept land. A king went mad and died. Another king succeeded him, and a princess named Victoria was born on the twenty-fourth of May in 1819.

When Napoleon appeared again, and other attempts by different people were made upon land acquisition and power exertion, there were wars and reports of wars.

Clanking steam engines were invented and built to run on rails. And the sky was red at night from the furnaces of the industrial Midlands. The furnaces and factories beckoned people from far and wide. Immigrant labour poured into the heart of England from overseas so that, in some of the places of work, it was not unusual to be alongside someone who spoke little English.

On the fourteenth of April 1819, the lamplighters' cry in the City of Birmingham underwent a change. When the darkness of night was approaching, the Birmingham Gas Light and Coke Company lit the streets with gas. The Leeries, as they came to light the lamps, adapted to the new brightness, singing *Daylight by night, A ha'peny for your safety*, and similar cries to inform the dwellers through whose streets they were walking of their presence.

Those whose streets were lit by gas found the change difficult to cope with. *We do not want this daytime brightness at night. We need the restful dark; our days are long and tiring.* A revolution was occurring, not by the spillage of blood. No, this revolution in the English

Midlands was happening due to the opening of thousands of industrial workshops, large and small, whose workers were engaged in manufacture and invention, clamouring to the forefront of world trade.

Some people rebelled against the change and how it would affect their lives. Groups of angry men, used to producing goods by hand, felt threatened by newly installed machinery. They thought the buzzing, whirling wood and iron monsters would destroy their livelihood, so they attacked them with hammers and fire. The working conditions in places of manufacture where owners thought more of money than their workpeople were harsh and demeaning.

Rebel. Let us rebel, went up the cry.

We work so hard for our families, they shouted. *And our work is taken from us by this infernal machinery.*

The oppressed in France demonstrated how to rise against oppression. But in England, a man stepped up to achieve better working conditions for mill workers without the use of extreme violence. Ned Ludd was his name. Employers felt unrest was intense in the air when he attempted to speak to them on behalf of his colleagues. When that failed, Ned Ludd's followers, the Luddites, put their desires into action and smashed up machinery.

Fear was in the minds of those in charge. *How far will this rebellion go?* Asked one employer of another. *If we are not careful, the guillotine may yet be used,* was the answer, so the army was called in. Some of the Luddites were hanged. Some were transported to Australia, and the unrest was quietened.

Those who lost their employment due to the new machinery did manage to find other work. And the cost of clothing fell dramatically due to less financial outlay paying people to produce it, which helped the finances of those who had felt oppressed and were earning a pittance. The undercurrent of conversation was sometimes about how to improve working conditions, some of which were harsh and desperate, even involving children, some of them under ten years of age.

* * *

In the Black Country, due to his services to the king and country in manufacturing agricultural and military accoutrements, Thomas Satchwell, the elderly owner of the Sampson Ironworks, was raised to the nobility, becoming Lord Satchwell of Halveston. On the night of his return from London as a member of the peerage, he had a visitor.

There was a hefty knock on the front door at Stourton Hall. The servant who opened the door recognised the visitor.

"Mister Makepeace, how are you?" asked the servant.

"I am well. How are you, William?"

"A trifle older than when I last saw you, sir. However, can I help you?"

"I would like to see Thomas Satchwell, if I may."

Certainly sir. Lord Satchwell and his wife are in the drawing room. Please step inside."

When Daniel Makepeace entered the drawing room, he saw Tom Satchwell and approached him, hand outstretched. "It's good to see you, Thomas." They shook.

"And it is good to see you, Daniel. What brings you here?" Thomas looked at Daniel, who was dressed in the uniform of a Captain of the 64th Regiment of Foot. He was taller than when they last met and had an air of authority.

When they were seated, the servant, William, offered drinks, and Thomas asked Daniel about his rise to the rank of Captain.

"I would prefer to tell you why I have come here." And Daniel told them about him and Joseph joining the army and going to fight in America.

"Joss took your spade, Tom. He wanted something to remember you by."

"It was he who took it? Where is he now, the coward, running away with my apprentice piece?"

"He longed to be back here, Tom. I buried him with your spade after he was killed. And his last word before the bullet took him was . . . *Father*."

Chapter 22

1820-1822

To the Heart of England

Amos Washington and his wife Katherine, a dressmaker, lived rent-free in the house first occupied on the Dumanoir estate by the previous head gardener, Jacob Taylor, and his wife, Myra. Myra died, some said, of a broken heart, just under a year after her husband.

Amos wanted a change. Being young at heart and adventurous in spirit, it teased his mind that, in the Midlands, new horizons were beckoning, and he mentioned this to Kate.

"There is a call for people of our age. By all accounts, factories produce all manner of goods in the Midlands. Industrial barons like Marcel Dumanoir build great houses from their new wealth in the middle shires. They are bound to need gardeners with my experience. And I am a carpenter too, and you have the dressmaker skills."

Kate was silent until Amos prompted her for a reply. "Yes, I would like a change, too," she said. "But it would be a big step to change our abode. Would you be able to obtain landscape or carpentry work?"

"For a certainty." Amos was confident of the outcome. "And we have savings to support us for at least a year.

"How would we travel?"

"By Stagecoach. There would be stops for the change of horses. The journey would take about two days, and we would stay overnight at the Golden Cross in Oxford. I have talked to Henry Wright, who owns the Carriage Company. Wright has lodgings, The Vixen Inn, in Birmingham, where he has his stables. He owns the place and has said we can rent two rooms in the yard."

"Two days is a long time to be travelling in discomfort."

"It is, but if we sacrifice comfort for two days to attain a new opportunity, it will be worth it."

The season was late autumn. With the weather likely to be inclement in the coming months, Amos and Katherine decided to delay moving to Birmingham until springtime. The spring season would be pleasant for their move and not beset with frost and snow.

Amos regularly contacted Henry Wright about work in Birmingham in the months they waited. Due to his carriage and transport work, Wright had contacts in Birmingham and on the route between Birmingham and Portsmouth. Moreover, Wright had a persuasive voice and could use his comprehensive store of vocabulary for his benefit and that of others.

Amos Washington's skills had impressed three of Wright's business acquaintances, and they wanted to meet him.

"Amos has important work to complete before he can travel from Portsmouth," Wright told them, which made employers eager to interview a person with so many skills.

April 9th 1821

Katherine awoke early on Monday. She had an intense air of excitement. "Amos, wake up . . . awake now." She woke as the sun rose and the first bird call piped through the open window. "Today is our day, my love." She felt like she was a young girl again with the brightest future.

"Yes, a fresh start." Amos raised his arms in the air and laughed. Then, he leapt out of bed, held her in his arms, and she felt safe. Finally, she was ready to face a world different from anything she had experienced in Portsmouth, the town of her birth. Katherine glanced at the clock, forty minutes past the hour of five. The coach would leave at half of the hour past seven.

* * *

The gentle rhythm of the horses' hooves was tiring and lulled Kate into an hour's sleep. She awoke and glanced out of the window she sat by. "See, there is a light yonder," Kate nudged Amos and pointed to the horizon, where there was gentle luminescence. Amos glanced at his pocket watch, barely illuminated by the light of the carriage lamp. It was just over two hours after sunset.

"Ten of the clock," he said. "That must be the town of Oxford." Amos felt cramped and wanted to stand, but with the other passengers vying for space, too, he had to be content with the room available. "A little while longer, Kate, and we can rest for the night."

They spent the night at the Golden Cross in Oxford. Then, starting early next day, they made unhindered progress toward Birmingham, with the final of many changes of horses at The Windmill Inn in Spon Street, Coventry.

"I think we've arrived," said Amos, as the coachman reined the horses back before urging them through a tall stone-built arch into a gas-lit courtyard.

"Oh look, Amos, there's Henry Wright," said Katherine. She saw his rotund figure standing below the sign of an inn, The Vixen, swinging in a freshening breeze. She had worried that the place where they would live would be a slum, but her fears were unfounded. The house, with stables to its right, looked perfect.

The coach rattled over the courtyard cobbles and drew to a halt. Wright had a ruddy complexion, although there was a distinct chill in the air. He came to the left-hand door of the coach and opened it. "You have kept good time, George. A quarter before the midnight hour," he called to the coachman. Wright was well known for taking personal responsibility for the well-being of his passengers, and he had been waiting for the coach to arrive.

"Welcome to Birmingham's Digbeth, one and all," he said merrily. His voice resounded above the panting and snorting horses.

"Into the taproom, come, come. Restore yourselves with a glass or two of grog after your long ride. Follow me." The coachman and the guard helped the outside passengers descend from the coach's top. Although it was April, they were chilled to the bone and were grateful for the offer of grog and the warmth of a roaring fire at the inn where they would spend the night.

"Amos . . . Amos and Katherine. It is good to see you in Birmingham. How was the travel?" Wright pointed to a table where they could sit.

"It was relatively comfortable," responded Katherine, "Although what it would be like in wintertime with snow on the lanes, I hate to consider." Amos nodded his agreement.

"The roads have improved greatly over the past ten years, but there is still much room for improvement," Henry Wright said. "I have heard that a man named Stephenson is tinkering around with steam power for a vehicle on some sort of track in a place called Stockton, but I doubt that will ever succeed."

"Time will tell. Boulton and Watt have made great progress providing steam power for mills and other factories."

"Yes, they have, but making a vehicle move along a track. That is very different." Henry pushed his thick-lensed glasses higher up his nose. "However, is it a measure or two of grog for you both, or would you like something lighter, maybe tea?" Henry asked Katherine.

"Our lives are full of change, Henry, so I will try the grog. Who knows, Stephenson may make a journey from Portsmouth to Birmingham take one day rather than two, and he may remove the expense of an overnight stay at a coaching inn." Sometimes Kate came straight to the point. Henry swiftly poured himself a glass of amber-coloured liquid.

He poured the same into two other glasses and picked up a water carafe. He was going to add it to Katherine's drink, but she placed her hand on his to stop him from watering the rum down. "I will take it unadulterated," she said firmly.

He looked at her. "You are a girl after my own heart," he stated, taking a large sip from his glass. He changed the subject. "Amos, you have three offers of work, all relating to your experience."

Although tired from the journey, Amos was immediately alert. "What are the offers?"

"They are subject to an interview, of course, but the first offer is as a carpenter at the Regency Carriage Works. Mister Steven Sant is the owner, and he is the person who would interview you.

There is an offer from the Birmingham Canal Boat Company. They need carpenters for their boat-building work. They are also considering making a canal barge using iron plates. The other offer is as head gardener at the premises of Josiah Simkin. He has a factory where he makes wooden wheels for carriages."

"Thank you for your help, Henry. Which of these would you think best?" Wright paused in thought and rested his chin on his hand. "If I had your skills and were as young as you, I would be tempted with the Birmingham Canal Boat Company offer. Iron plating for boats may be the way forward." Amos nodded. He stood and held out his hand for Kate. "I am inclined to agree. Can we talk about this tomorrow? We have been awake for many hours, and sometimes the going has been rough and unsteady."

"Of course. I'm glad to oblige. I will ask Jones to see you to your room." He stood. Henry Wright's wife had died some years back. He had no close family and felt somewhat attached to Amos and Katherine. "Oh, Amos," he called after them. "I have work for you as well if you want it. The walled garden at the rear of these buildings belongs to me. You see, The Vixen was my wife's property. I want the land maintained to provide food for the inn. And since you are a carpenter, you could also maintain my coaches."

Ianto Jones led them by candlelight up to their room. Candles were alight on the mantel and the dressing table. A fire in the hearth was low, but, as tired as they were, they added another few logs, which caught and gave a welcome glow and warmth to the room, which had large blackened timbers from bygone years in the ceiling and walls.

"We have choices before us, Amos," said Kate. She had brought the remnants of her glass of rum up with her, and she took a sip, smiled and then laughed. "I love you, Amos," she said. "Are you happy with our new station in life? You have the offer of work. I am a dressmaker, and people always need new clothes or repairs to their existing wardrobe." He put his finger gently on her lips.

"And regardless of all those other things, I love you, Katherine Washington."

Chapter 23

1822-1845

In Digbeth, and Then to Warwick

They awoke late the following day. Ianto Jones was in the bar area, and the smell of bacon hung in the air and tempted the appetite. The other stagecoach passengers were at breakfast, and there were cheerful comments about the start of the day, the sun being bright and full of promise.

"Please be seated," said Ianto, guiding Amos and Katherine to a table by a window overlooking the garden Henry Wright mentioned the previous night. It was large and situated in a walled area but overgrown with weeds and brambles.

Amos stood and moved to the window to survey the extent of the walled garden. "Much work must be done to make that land useable," he told Ianto. "I think the offer of work from the Birmingham Canal Boat Company may be the best. As a ship's carpenter, I have all the skills needed. Also, my sea-going experience has much to offer regarding endurance."

"Henry said they are also experimenting with Iron plating for the boats."

"That is interesting. Iron boats, indeed."

Amos Washington was successful with his interview. He became employed as a Master Carpenter at the Birmingham Canal Boat Company at their wharf at Digbeth Junction. In the days preceding the interview, Amos tried to learn about an iron boat's ability to float.

115

Then, in a moment of exasperation, he approached Ianto Jones, who was a knowledgeable man by the manner of his speaking, albeit with a strong Welsh accent.

"Do you know if iron floats, Ianto?"

"As a lump of iron, it does not float, boyo. It rather depends upon the shape of the iron as to whether it floats. Any object, when placed in water, displaces its own weight of water. Now, if the object is hollow, like a boat, whatever it is made of, either wood or iron, it displaces more water than its own weight, making it float."

"Ah, is that so? Where did you learn that?"

"It is one of the things about being an Innkeeper that you learn things from many different people. For example, I learned about buoyancy from a man who teaches the sciences at the University of Cambridge."

* * *

In his office, the Birmingham Canal Boat Company owner, Andrew Fielding, asked Amos to describe how to make a cross-halving joint. Then Fielding reached into his desk drawer and handed Amos two lengths of wood, each nine inches long. "Tell me, Mister Washington, what variety of wood is this?" Amos scanned the grain, the silvery cast and the attractive pattern of the medullary rays. "It is oak, sir, without a doubt."

"Follow me, and bring the wood." Fielding led Amos to a workshop where several men were working, some at benches working on individual components. Others were working on the framework of a long, narrow boat inside some closed wooden doors with windows. Outside was a slipway sloping down to the canal of Digbeth Junction.

Fielding indicated a vacant workbench with a wooden vice and a selection of woodworking tools. "I will leave you here for a while, Mister Washington. Using those two lengths of oak, I want you to make a cross-halving joint. When you have completed it, bring it to my office."

The tools were good quality, the chisels newly sharpened, and within a half hour, Amos was back in Fielding's office with his demonstration piece. It was tightly constructed, perfectly square and level.

Fielding cast his eyes over it. "That is a well-made piece. I have another question about boats. The material used to make them is wood, but iron is far stronger. It is also far heavier. Do you think an iron boat could float?" It was as if his conversation with Ianto Jones was pre-destined for this occasion. Amos gave his explanation.

"Very well, sir, you may leave now," said the boatyard owner. He was holding the cross-halving joint, feeling the surface of the wood. He felt no difference in the level of the two surfaces.

As Amos was about to leave the office, Fielding called after him, "Mister Washington, this is a well-constructed joint. Also, you are the only man who has applied for this post and was able to answer the question about buoyancy. Well done, sir; I look forward to having you in our employ. You may start work on Monday next."

And thus, it took place. On Monday next, a day that was overcast and mizzling with rain, Amos began work in the covered dry dock at Digbeth Junction.

Katherine waved him off and decided how to organise her day. First, she would go to shops in the area and put a note in their window telling of her availability to make dresses and coats and repair clothes for a moderate price.

* * *

It was evening time in their lodgings at The Vixen. Amos' first day at Digbeth Wharf went well. He told Katherine how two blacksmiths used small iron objects called rivets. They fixed large iron plates together and fastened them onto cast iron frames to form the hull of the canal boat, which would be called a 'barge'.

"It is a time-consuming process and very noisy. The rivets are heated in a brazier until red-hot and hammered into holes in the overlapping iron plates to join them. During a break for lunch, I spoke to the blacksmiths. They said that when the rivets cool, their length shrinks, which draws the iron plates together tightly. They *fuller* the edges of the plates to close the metal together and make the joints watertight."

"Very interesting, I am sure."

"Yes. I hope it will be watertight when the company launch the barge and people are aboard her."

"Will you learn to work with the mix of iron and wood?"

"I have started to do that. During the afternoon, Andrew Fielding asked me to join the blacksmiths and help them."

Kate related to Amos about finding four shops nearby whose owners had allowed her to put a note in their window telling of her work as a dressmaker and seamstress. "One of the shop owners asked if I would make one of his coats larger, and his wife, an amply-shaped woman, wants me to make her a dress. I am to return tomorrow to take their measurements."

"Then today in Birmingham has been good for us both."

* * *

It took three months to complete the iron hull. The launch day coincided with another event. All over the nation, bunting was out, bands were playing, and a different future lay ahead. The crowning of young Queen Victoria of the House of Hanover occurred on the twenty-eighth of June, 1838.

At Digbeth Junction, a crowd gathered around the basin to witness the launching of *Goliath* as the barge was to be named. Katherine was there with Amos, who helped construct the iron hull and make and fit the interior woodwork. The Goliath was to be a passenger-carrying canal barge pulled by a Shire horse called *David*.

The passengers, for a fee, would be towed along the Digbeth Branch Canal. The doors of the boatyard opened, and the crowd grew quiet as they saw the gleaming reds and greens of the barge. And then they cheered as a Tangye pump pushed the boat onto the slipway. Chains held it fast, poised and ready for release down the wooden supports and into the water of Digbeth Junction.

Amos grasped Kate's hand and felt her skin was slightly rough. His hand moved about hers, touching it gently. "Your hand is not as smooth as it used to be," he said.

"You have been so busy with your new work on the barge that you haven't noticed the walled garden," she said.

"Why, what's happened to it?" Kate had deliberately not told Amos how she had been working on the land. She wanted it to be a surprise, an achievement of her own using the spade he insisted would come with them from

Portsmouth. She enjoyed working on the land more, she realised, than she wanted her sewing work.

Amos looked at her hands, hardened at the base of her fingers. "I am sorry, Kate. I must look at what you have done when we get back. Wear gloves when you work on the land and put cream on your hands." He squeezed her hand gently just as Andrew Fielding commanded to slip the chain, which began to unwind off a large pulley.

Goliath gathered speed. A great splash occurred as it reached the water. The brake was applied, and the iron-hulled boat lay gently rocking in Digbeth Junction. A cheer arose from the crowd, some of whom had travelled miles to see the launch of an iron boat. Indeed, it was the beginning of a new age.

* * *

"You have done remarkably well, Kate." Amos praised his wife for her effort in the garden. In the far corner, a fire was smouldering. "The soil looks good."

"It digs easily."

"You have done very well, my Kate." Amos looked at Katherine. Her beautiful face, lithe physique, and her strength of character delighted him.

In time, they had a son who, as he developed, showed the same intuitiveness as his father for making things. How events and the onward progression of the inventive mind of man shape history and the lives of the individuals we become acquainted with.

Amos Washington had remarkable skills and the type of mind that enabled him, in a short space of years, to become one of the directors of the Birmingham Canal Boat Company.

His skill with the tools used to manipulate iron and his ability to design the interior of the barges soon came to Andrew Fielding's notice. Fielding was a progressive businessman. By his skills and business acumen, he had risen from the slums of Digbeth with nothing in the way of finance to be a well-respected member of society. With new acquaintances, he could detect their inner drive and desires. Honesty and dependability were what Fielding saw in Amos Washington's character, and they became firm friends.

Chapter 24

1845-1855

Jack Washington

"What are your thoughts about navigating Goliath to Warwick," asked Fielding. "There is a Mister Simeon Blackwell who is interested in having us build an iron-hulled barge similar to Goliath for pleasure use around the town of Warwick."

"I could navigate to Warwick. Such a trip is possible, and it would be an experience for Jack," Amos replied. "But I would not do the trip without Kate."

Jack, Amos and Kate's son, was a man of twenty-two years. He had a pleasant disposition, strength, and determination inherited from his father and mother. He tended the walled garden at the rear of their house, which was attached to The Vixen. The turn of good fortune with Amos becoming a Birmingham Canal Boat Company director enabled them to buy the property they previously rented. The attached walled garden, an acre in size, now had a heated glasshouse similar to the one Amos designed those crowding years ago at Chateau Dumanoir.

Under his father's tutelage, Jack Washington became a proficient carpenter. He built the glasshouse and supplied local taverns and hotels with fresh vegetables, milk and eggs from the cows and chickens that roamed the field at the rear of the walled garden.

Jack enjoyed working with the land. He loved the growth of his seedlings with their progress to maturity over the onward change of seasons.

A friend of his was the son of Ianto Jones. Dafydd Jones helped with the walled garden and the smallholding. Together, they sometimes walked along the canal towpath to a tavern near a farm put to agriculture and livestock. There, they met and discussed agricultural matters with the farmer, Ira Webb and his three sons.

As a result of these conversations, Jack and Dafydd became seriously interested in farming. They began spending eight hours every week helping on the farm and learning agriculture techniques.

On one occasion in the tavern, Brian, one of Webb's sons, was there on his own, and the conversation between him and Jack took on an ominous tone.

"Our farm is one in a thousand which have good working conditions. Most farm owners treat their workers little better than the animals," said Brian. "Our farm has been in the family for three generations. We take care of each other and our workers. So we make sure they are not worked to exhaustion, as are many labourers on the farms of England and Wales."

"How do you know that?"

"We are in contact with labourers on several farms. Father's brother is a farmer near Princethorpe, a village near Coventry. He is a cruel man to his workers. He prides himself on treating them as fodder. He even speaks openly and with humour about that."

"Surely that isn't common in this country," said Jack, thinking of the immigrant labour and progressive industry in Birmingham and the Black Country. He had heard whispers of child labour in some of the industrial mills but thought it was unfounded hearsay. But after listening to Brian's sincere words, he realised that widespread abuse did seem to be happening. After all, the government recruited young men to go onto battlefields and get slaughtered. So it stood to reason that some employers would use people cruelly to achieve financial gain.

Jack found it difficult to remove the conversation with Brian Webb from his mind. He was involved with agriculture, and his working conditions were near perfect. So the heartless situation facing agricultural labourers and their families hit Jack hard. When he lay in bed that night, he still heard Brian's voice speaking of the hardships that were facing some families. So to resolve his unsettled feeling, Jack met Webb again to find out more.

When they met, Brian looked around the bar to see if anyone was close enough to hear what he said. No one was nearby, but he still spoke in a whisper. "Jack, say nothing about where you heard this information."

"Most certainly. What you say is between you and me."

"Things are bad country-wide. But we have contact with people near my uncle's land at Princethorpe. Further down the lane toward Southam is a village called Barford, where a man lives who is like a general leading his troops. He is determined to improve working conditions. There's a farm I've heard about where workers' conditions are terrible. A family living there were suffering great hardship. The hovel where they lived had a mud floor. Filth surrounded them, and the man and his wife died of starvation. They had given their last scraps of food to their two children. It was stale bread, but the poor little mites were too young to be able to feed themselves, and they were found dead also, with the food in front of them."

The words had been disturbing. They created a wave of

deep anger in Jack that he hadn't experienced before. He was determined to learn more about the situation and do something about it. But he was uncertain what he could do.

The evening after the revelation by Brian Webb about the terrible working conditions experienced by agricultural labourers, Jack's father, Amos, mentioned the journey to Warwick on the iron barge, Goliath.

"Really, when?" was Jack's enthusiastic response. Amos looked at Kate to see how she responded and saw her smile.

"We can go any time we're ready," Amos said. "Such a journey would take us three and a half to four days and the same to return. If you agree to accompany me, Kate, the three of us could go. We could also spend two days in Warwick to have a break."

For Jack, this was like a heaven-sent opportunity. Men conversing in a tavern in the town of Warwick, a mere stone's throw from Barford, could give him information. Of course, he might have to go a few times until hearing a conversation about working conditions. But then he would be better positioned to decide what he could do.

* * *

The Shire horse, David, had towed the iron barge, Goliath, around most of Birmingham's expanding network of canals. David and the passenger boat, Goliath, had given many hundreds of people hours of pleasure. But David was now old and had recently been put to pasture. So a Suffolk Punch named Major towed Goliath to Warwick, being led, in turn, by Amos and Jack.

Shortly after mooring, Simeon Blackwell, the potential customer, arrived. After the Suffolk Punch towed Goliath along the towpath to Leamington and back to Warwick, Blackwell was enthusiastic.

"Yes . . . yes indeed. I am happy with this craft; the iron hull will need less maintenance than its wooden counterpart." They shook hands. Blackwell agreed to visit Digbeth Junction to review barge plans and discuss his internal layout requirements.

"We are having a break in Warwick for two days, but we'll return to the boatyard in the morning three days hence," suggested Amos. "You may return with us on Goliath if you wish." Blackwell readily agreed.

It was time for Jack to begin his mission to get information about agricultural workers' living conditions. He told Amos and Kate that he would explore Warwick and might be back late.

He went along the canal towpath to where a signpost saying *Warwick: 1/2 Mile* pointed to a footpath, which he followed. He came to a hilly street with many half-timbered buildings. A tall stone-built town gate with the road running through it was to his left. To the right, some fifty paces downhill, was an inn sign, The Tudor House, which should suit his purpose well.

A clock in the distance struck the hour of one as he strode down the street to the inn. On the way, he passed a youth selling newspapers, The Warwick and Warwickshire Advertiser. Rather than draw attention to himself sitting at a table for hours, drinking slowly and doing nothing else, he bought a newspaper to fill his time reading.

Typically, Jack, a tall, well-proportioned man due to the exercise of his agricultural work, would drink three pints of beer in an evening if he visited a tavern. Although it was not his favourite drink, being weak and under-flavoured, he chose small ale because he was determined to remain clear-headed.

During the afternoon, a young woman who looked about eighteen years of age came into the inn with an older man. They sat at a table next to Jack.

"Is it the usual, Guy?" the landlord called. Guy called back; *Make it a pint o' the best.*

"And you, Miss Thompson, what is yours today?"

"Dry sherry, if you please, Len."

"A single or a double?"

"A single."

The attractive Miss Thompson blew a strand of tawny-coloured hair away from her face and turned to look at Jack, just a glance, but it was enough to make Jack's heart skip a beat. He moved the newspaper to enable himself to see her better, and she smiled.

Just as Brian Webb's words were cast indelibly upon Jack's mind, so was Miss Thompson's smile. But the smile was captivating in an entirely different way. It possessed an essence of lasting beauty, which put Brian Webb's words, which contained an air of misery, into the background.

The landlord brought over the drinks for Guy and the beautiful Miss Thompson. Jack immediately stood, put his paper down and went to their table. "Please, sir and miss, let me buy the drinks for you," he said. Guy looked at him quizzically, and then his face creased into a smile.

"I thank you very much. That is kind of you. But please, come and sit with us."

Jack lifted his chair over. "What is your name?" Guy asked. Introductions were made, and Miss Thompson became Grace. Guy was Grace's father, and they had come by horse and cart from Sherbourne, where they had a smallholding. Guy became dejected when he told how his wife had died twelve months previously. Grace took her father's hand and stroked it gently. Jack saw her look of compassion, and, in a way, it harmonised with what he wanted to do for those in agriculture being downtrodden by the cruelties of their employers.

"I don't want to be forward, Mister Thompson, but . . ."

"Jack, call me Guy, please."

"Thank you . . . Guy," Jack smiled. "But have you heard anything locally about the desperate living conditions experienced by agricultural labourers and their families?"

Guy was surprised by the young man's comment. It came from the heart. "Are you involved with farm work?" he asked, and Jack explained his involvement with the smallholding and his skill with carpentry. Then, without hesitation, and to Jack's complete surprise, Guy told him that he could offer him well-paid work and the chance of advancement. "Initially, you would need to work alongside our other workers to gain their confidence and that of other labourers in the area. But, you see, there is other work I would like you to do. I know you would find it interesting and, from what you have said, I am sure you would find it very satisfying.

Chapter 25

1855-1868

Sherbourne

Jack Washington moved to Sherbourne to work at the farm owned by Guy Thompson. Jack's mother and father were saddened by their son's decision to move from Digbeth. Still, they were happy that their son, who had spoken about his feelings for Grace Thompson, had thoughts about marriage and having his own family.

"You had better take this spade as you are going to work on the land," said Amos, handing the implement to his son the evening before Jack left. Amos had cleaned the spade up before he took it into the house. The ash handle was well-seasoned, and he had rubbed the wood with whale oil. As a result, it had a golden sheen when it dried.

"I'll take care of it, dad," Jack reassured his father.

"I am sure you will. But you take care of yourself and Grace. She's a good girl, very caring." Amos and Kate had met her and Guy in Warwick, and as they talked about these intimate things, Jack noticed that his father's eyes looked moist. Father and son were close.

"The railway line now connects Birmingham to Warwick and Leamington. So, Jack, if you moved further away than Sherbourne, we could visit each other by train," said Kate.

* * *

The Thompson farmland was bordered on one side by some woodland near Sherbourne Park and on the other side by the River Avon. The house was stone and timber-built, with the timber framework blackened with age.

Jack Washington arrived on foot, having walked with his spade resting on his shoulder from Warwick. Including Jack, there were three workers at the farm and a working family of three, parents and a two-year-old boy. The workers lived in various outbuildings in a courtyard opposite the large house.

Guy Thompson had been impressed with how Jack had approached him at The Tudor House Inn. The young man was confident and not shy about talking to him and Grace about a subject causing concern about the plight of agricultural workers and their families. On many farms in Great Britain, the conditions workers and their families had to endure were criminally oppressive. Guy Thompson's concern grew from an experience when he was a youngster.

His parents died in tragic circumstances, so he was told, but the cause was never revealed. He was six years old when it happened, and a neighbour, Eva Black, whose husband had died some years previously, took him in and fed and housed him. He was forced to do menial tasks for most of the day. The house was a little better than a pig sty, and relief for Guy came with gardening.

There was land at the front and back of the cottage. Young Guy spent what hours he could in the back garden, near an attractive spinney to which he escaped and made a den within a thicket of trees. Guy whiled away his time in the shelter, observing birds, insects, plants and trees. As time passed, he grew to love being close to the wild things and noted the times and seasons when plants grew from seedlings, came to fruition and died.

When he was twelve, Guy made up his mind and decided to leave the life of struggle as the woman's skivvy.

One spring night, when the moon was full, and a nightingale was piping his heart out, young Guy stole out of the filthy house. He was determined to better himself and, if possible, to better the lives of others. He made that his goal in life. Even in his tender years, Guy pitied Eva Black despite the menial tasks she forced him to do. Some nights he had heard her sobbing in her bedroom. She had fed him and allowed him a bed to sleep in, and maybe, if it was possible to make his way in the world, Guy determined to return one day and help her. So he left.

He walked down the lane lit by the moon in the direction of Warwick. When he reached the town, he crossed the bridge over a wide river and wandered along a street at the side of Warwick Castle. Finally, he came to a road with many houses and a timber-framed inn with a door deeply set into the building enough to shelter him.

When he awoke early the following day, he realised how alone he was. Passers-by took no notice of him, and then a middle-aged gentleman with distinctive white hair walked by and then returned. "Are you alright, my lad?" he asked, entering the porch and bending down with a concerned look.

Guy had not experienced that sort of concern in his short life, and it made him break down in tears. But then, the gentleman came close and held him in his arms.

"There, there. Never mind," the man said. "Tell me about it." Young Guy opened his heart and released all the tension. When he told the gentleman, who turned out to be Professor Sir Denton Stokes, about why he came to be in the doorway. "Tell you what, sunshine, you come home with me. I am sure my wife would love to meet you."

So Guy went home with the Professor by private

carriage to a lovely townhouse in Stratford-upon-Avon. On the way to the Professor's home, the gentleman asked about Guy's interests. The lad spoke about plants, how to grow them, and the animals he had seen in the wild woodland.

When they reached the Professor's home, Guy felt the warmth of the welcome given by Martha, Lady Stokes.

"Guy, call me Auntie Martha," she said. There had been a brief explanation about how her husband had come across the lad. The kindly-looking woman's voice reminded Guy of his mother, a shadowy figure who left his life long ago.

Denton Stokes, Uncle Den, and Guy became very close as time passed. The Professor and his wife had been unable to have children, and young Guy had come into their lives at the right time.

The Professor was a lecturer at the Royal College of Agriculture in Cirencester, so when Guy reached the age of entry, he started at the college and eventually obtained a degree in Agricultural Science.

However, his early years were indelibly printed upon his mind. On the evening he left the home of Eva Black, the resolve he made that he would better the lives of those who suffer remained with him. After Guy set up his farm, with the financial help of Professor Sir Denton Stokes, he did return to Eva Black's house. He had some workmen clean the place up, and after a few months, he invited the woman he now called Aunt Eva to live in a small farmworker's cottage on his land.

* * *

At their first meeting in The Tudor House Inn, Guy Thompson recognised the instant communication between his daughter, Grace and Jack Washington. It was the same when Guy and his late wife, Eleanor, first set eyes on each other; there was an instant attraction.

When Jack spoke about his concern for the farm labourers' lot in life, Guy's first thought was that he and Jack could work together to improve their situation. So that instant attraction between Grace and Jack conveniently began the process. But Guy was not by nature a mercenary character. On the contrary, he intended to allow the passage of time to prove that Grace and Jack's relationship would be long-lasting and that Jack could be trusted.

Over several years Guy Thompson had thought through a plan about infiltrating a farm where cruelty was happening. Evidence would be gathered to bring about prosecution, which would be made public. In Guy's mind, equally determined to put matters right, Jack Washington brought the plan closer to happening.

They would have to work secretly to get information about the cruelties experienced by farm workers and those responsible for the suffering. It would be a long project. For it to succeed, Jack would have to learn farming techniques until they were second nature, so he could blend in with other farm labourers.

The work, and their friendship, went well for Jack and Guy, and the romance between Grace and Jack blossomed. They married, and after three years, their family had increased by two children, a boy and a girl.

His first two years on Guy's farm were like an apprenticeship. Jack was taught how to set a two-wheeled plough for the desired width and depth of furrow. And, far more complicated, he learned how to guide the two Suffolk Punch horses pulling the plough. First, the furrow horse, Amber and the land horse, Tawny, were steered toward a spot on the far hedge. Before long, Jack could turn them accurately, and his furrows were straight.

But he also used his carpentry and ironwork skills on carriage and building repair work. As a result, he gained the respect and confidence of his workmates, the farm labourers, and their employers on nearby and more distant farms. Landowners realised they could approach Guy Thompson and Jack Washington to get repairs done on their premises, which was precisely what Guy wanted.

"Jack, I need to speak to you alone," said Guy one afternoon, "It's a subject of great importance." They agreed to meet at seven o'clock that evening.

Jack wondered what was coming as he approached Guy's end of the large building where they all lived, with sensible separation. With Guy Thompson now in his sixty-third year, he appreciated the nearness of his daughter and Jack.

"You are doing well, Jack. You are an exceptional worker and a good son-in-law," he said after handing Jack a jug of stout. They drank to each other's health, and Jack wondered what would follow.

"Do you remember our conversation when we first met?"

"As if it was yesterday,"

"Well, let's return to the terrible working conditions of agricultural workers your friend told you about."

"Brian Webb. He was the son of a farm owner."

Walter nodded. "Then, no doubt you have noticed that the conditions for our workers are excellent on my farm."

"I have. Credit is due to you for doing that."

"It comes from my experience when I was young. I'll tell you about that sometime, but I want to tell you my plan. I intend to collaborate with a man living in the nearby village of Barford."

Jack's curiosity was aroused.

"The man's name is Joseph Arch."

"I've heard of him from farm labourers I've been in contact with."

"I am sure you have. Joseph Arch's fame is spreading. But Jack, when I first met you in The Tudor House Inn, I recognised that your passion for working conditions is the same as mine and Joe Arch."

"This is getting interesting."

"Yes. Because of the feeling you've expressed, I've assumed that you would be prepared to work with me to better the lives of agricultural workers."

"That is certainly true."

"So I had to develop a plan. First, I would need someone I could trust who would want to work with me. Time had to go by to prove that. Jack, I have come to love you as a son." Jack reached out and held Guy's arm for a second or so.

His father-in-law continued, "For my plan to work, I would need someone to work with me who was familiar with all manner of farm work. However, I perceived a problem from how you spoke when we met. Although skilled in various trades, you had little farm work experience."

"At the time, I was spending a day a week helping on Webb's farm, learning the ropes, so to speak."

Guy nodded. "I hope you don't mind, Jack, but I've been planning what we will do. Setting the scene, so to speak."

"What is your plan, Guy?"

"We need to infiltrate one of the farms where conditions are appalling to gather evidence. The work you have been doing here has prepared you to go onto one of those farms. If you gained extensive farm work experience, that action would become possible. Jack, I have prepared you for this only because I know how much you want to improve those poor people's working conditions. I'll tell you this: I would have done the investigation myself if I was young enough and knew what I know now. I hope you don't feel used?"

"Used? Most certainly not, privileged, more like."

Jack was intrigued by the plan. Since he had been living in Sherbourne, he had an inkling that there might be more to his work with Guy Thompson than was apparent. There had been direction in the work he was doing. When Jack's family and Guy had an evening meal together, his father-in-law would ask him how his work was doing as if it was a test. Jack had the patience to wait, to see what would occur. Excitement gripped him as Guy continued.

"There is a wealthy farm owner near the village of Ratley. Grantham Cripps is a knight of the realm known for his penny-pinching ways and how he keeps his workers and their families in poverty. Most of them were born into the farming way of life. They desperately need work, and they can't improve their situation."

"Why are you interested in this Grantham Cripps man?"

"He is similar to many landowners country-wide who take advantage of their workers' inability to escape oppressive working conditions. As a result, those poor people are treated little better than animals."

Jack Washington's face became grim. "So we'll fight a strategic action."

"We will, but without weapons. So you see, if you are willing, because there may be an element of danger, you will go in as a spy."

"I am more than willing. When do we start?"

* * *

Over the following weeks, Jack and Grace sometimes discussed what would happen.

"Please do not endanger yourself, Jack," she said. Her voice was firm. She had a quality that endeared her to Jack. Grace was so forthright, vital in a beautifully feminine way that entwined with Jack's strength of character.

They both wanted a better world for those who were downtrodden. Although Grace didn't want her husband to put himself in danger, she would not stand in his way if he could help those less fortunate than themselves.

Eva Black, who took Guy Thompson into her house when his parents died, was now in her eighty-fifth year. Over time, her mind had mellowed, mainly due to the help she got from Guy. Finally, Eva could let go of the cruelty her husband put her through before he left her. Sometimes she sat with Grace and Jack, passing the time in pleasant conversation. Eva spent the occasional evening with the children while Grace and Jack went for a walk. And now she was drawn into the plan to help agricultural workers, which did her heart good.

"Yes, of course I'll help," she said. She still tried to make reparation for how she demanded tasks from Guy when he was young. "Before my days are out, I want to see the world a better place for people like my nephew. He was a farm worker too, and he died of typhoid in a house unsuitable for a pig-sty."

The day eventually arrived for the plan to begin.

"Please take care, Jack," Grace said. Jack gently wiped the tear from her cheek.

"Don't worry, I will avoid danger," Jack reassured her.

Chapter 26

1868-1872

Cripps of Ratley and Joseph Arch

The horse and cart stopped at the bottom of the steep incline leading to Edgehill village. The clandestine thirteen-mile journey had been planned with much forethought.

"For this to work We must never be seen as associates," Jack stressed to his father-in-law before they bade farewell.

"Yes. So shall we meet as strangers at the Rose and Crown in Ratley," Guy said.

"Much like we did in Warwick."

"Aye. And there, you can inform me of what you observe."

"Shall we meet a week today, at noon on Sunday, in the Rose and Crown? And Guy, bring Grace. If you don't, I will not be part of this." Jack looked serious.

Guy smiled. "I'll bring her. Anyhow, gathering the evidence to make life uncomfortable for those responsible shouldn't take too long. I've said this before, but I mean it. You're a good man, Jack Washington. I think that between us, we'll improve the lot of the farm workers."

Jack nodded and swung himself off the cart.

"Goodbye, son," Guy tapped the horse with his whip, urged it to turn and waved farewell.

* * *

On the left, a little way up the hilly cart track to Edgehill, a finger-post with the name 'Ratley' pointed down a footpath. With his spade and meagre possessions, Jack made his way along it. He had allowed his hair to become unkempt, hadn't washed for over two weeks, and looked suitably desperate for work.

Cripps' farmland lay half a mile down the lane going past Ratley church. As Jack walked along the track, the stone-built manor Guy described came into view on raised ground to the right, and to the left of the manor was a lane leading to the farmland. Barns and low brick and wood buildings were arranged around three sides of a large yard.

Jack took the left turn. The lane leading to the house and the one to the farm buildings were starkly different. The one to the house was made of compressed crushed stone, whilst the track to the farm was mud, rutted by the wheels of carts. When he was halfway along the path, the door of a wooden shack up ahead swung open, and a man with a shotgun stepped out. "What do you want?" he called out firmly as he stepped into the centre of the track.

"I need work. Can I see the manager?"

"What d'you do?"

"Anything available," Jack said as he approached the man. "Apart from hedge-laying."

"Wait here." The man walked toward the outhouses, at the end of which was a two-storey building. He knocked on a door and walked in. A short while later, he came out and told Jack to enter the office.

The interview was short and to the point. Jack was told by the estate manager, Reuben Ellis, that he could help dig and maintain ditches and culverts for drainage around the perimeter of Cripps' fields. "We need four men to do this work. One died last week, so you've come at the right time.

Our man will show you to your room."

The man he had met had the gun crooked open on his arm and indicated for Jack to follow him. He introduced himself as Edward Guphill. "I'm one of the gamekeepers here and a general dogsbody. We gamekeepers man the blockhouse for a day each, turn-by-turn," Guphill went into one of the wooden buildings with rudimentary furniture and a curtain as a room divider.

Jack noted the worn layout, the strong animal smell, and the floor, which was earth, with distinct hoofmarks. A child's game was on the table, and a football was on the floor.

Guphill led the way up some stairs to the attic room.

"Here we are. Here's your place." There was a bed, a deal table with a chair, an open grate with the ashes from the last fire, a rail with clothes hanging on it, and a cupboard with a wash bowl and a large jug of water.

"Is what you call the blockhouse the shack you came out of with a gun?"

Guphill sat on the chair. Put the shotgun on the table. "Yes, that's the blockhouse. Anyway, Jack, you begin work at six tomorrow morning. Finish at six in the evening. You will earn seven shillings and sixpence a week." Guphill told Jack the costs that would be deducted from his wages. "One and six for this room. The food you will be provided with, bread, cheese, bacon, sugar and three pints of cider a day, will cost two and sixpence a week and fuel for your fire is two shillings a week." Jack noticed that Guphill grimaced, and he did a quick mental calculation. The money he would be left with for clothes and enjoyment would be one and six a week, which, fortunately, he wasn't dependent on.

"Thanks, Ed. You don't mind me calling you Ed, do you?"

"That's alright. I get called all manner of things."

Jack smiled and went over to the bed. It was reasonably soft, but the bedding was dirty. He looked at Guphill.

"You mentioned bacon; who does the cooking, us?"

"There's a family of three living below, Philip and Mary Redgrave and their son, Jonas. He's an eight-year-old. Mary does the cooking for the workers. She cooks well."

"That'll help a starving man," Jack rubbed his stomach. "Ed, did this room of mine belong to the man who died?"

"It did. Simon was a nice young chap."

"What happened to him?"

Guphill stood up. "Why do you want to know?"

"I'm in his room. There are his clothes. What do I do, burn them or bury them?"

Guphill sat again and breathed deeply. "He was the sort of man who kept himself to himself. I know things were getting difficult for him. Simon had an elderly mother in Wellesbourne who he tried to help. But his health failed him, and he coughed a great deal. He probably had tuberculosis. But I've said enough. You be careful, Jack. Work well, and you'll be alright."

Guphill left, and Jack sat in the chair, considering his situation. It had been a long and tense day, and although early, he drifted off to sleep.

* * *

Breakfast consisted of flour mixed with butter to which water was added. A little bread was shared out and taken to eat as lunch. The ditching work was hard and laborious. The fields extended over many acres. Each area drained into a ditch that fed into the nearby River Avon. The ditches often needed debris clearing, particularly in wintertime when ditching was a never-ending task. The first one was started again, as the last one was cleared.

The spade given to Jack by his father was sharp, cutting through weeds and roots quickly. The working day was long and hard, cold and wet, with a short break at midday to eat their bread. After their day's work, the other three men were as tired as Jack. One of them, Titus Ingram, and Jack struck an immediate friendship. He was a forty-year-old. Titus had a good sense of humour, and although the work was hard, the man was light-hearted throughout the day. His mood lightened the effort needed to keep working.

It was getting dark. In the distance, there was the faint sound of a bell. "That's it, we finish now, and we eat," called Ralph, the gang leader, from further along the ditch. Jack wiped his spade on some grass, joined the others, and they made their way back to the outbuildings a half mile away.

It had become evident to Jack during the working day how close the men were as friends. Although they were tired and strolled back to their lodgings at a leisurely pace, they chatted amicably and with humour.

"Come to my room tonight if you like, Titus," said Jack, "I've brought some ale with me." Titus's eyes brightened.

The Ditchers, as the four called themselves, entered the building where the smell of bacon was strong. A woman was at the stove, forking bacon in a large pan. A second large saucepan was boiling with potatoes and carrots. The woman glanced at Jack and Titus as they entered.

"You're the new man above?" she asked.

"I am. Jack Washington's the name. I'm told your cooking's good. It smells delicious," she smiled. Jack noted her careworn look, but her smile and hair had the appearance of a woman only in her late twenties.

A man wearing a smock was sitting at the table. A boy sitting on his lap was toying with the game pieces. They both looked exhausted. The man raised his hand to Jack and Titus. "You alright?" he asked.

"So-so. Ready to eat," Titus replied. "Thank you, Mary; smells good. There's a room next door, Jack. That's where we eat. Follow me."

The food was good, but there was little to feed the nineteen workers, men, women and some children. The conversation tended to be gloomy. There was no laughter. As soon as the food was eaten, the people left the room. Most of the men were in smocks, which were torn and patched. His gaze followed them, and he felt saddened and angry.

Titus saw Jack looking at the people. "Up to your place now, Jack?"

"Yes." Jack collected the nearby plates and cutlery. "Where do you want these, Mary?" he called. She looked surprised.

"Well, sir, through this door to the sink in our room, if you will."

* * *

"You seem well educated, Jack, and thoughtful," said Titus as Jack raked the ashes from the fire and placed kindling on the paper. He struck a Lucifer match and added logs once the kindling was alight.

"I had a good teacher," Jack said, going to his chair. He hadn't anticipated what Titus would say next.

"Your clothes are good. However, they are not befitting your work in the ditches." Jack and Guy had rehearsed answers to possible questions they could be asked, but they hadn't thought of this one. So Jack invented an answer he hoped would work.

"They were on a washing line a few nights back, and I slept in the garden shed." Titus seemed satisfied with the answer, and then,

"We do struggle here. It's hard." But we have no choice. "What do you think after your first day?"

Jack took a swig of ale from his bottle.

"I've had a hard time," Jack said. "When I was working down in Wiltshire, the conditions were bad. The landowner went to London for a while and came back with cholera. He and some of his workers died, and the place was shut down. That was three months ago. I've been living off the land ever since."

"You didn't catch cholera?" Titus took drunk some ale.

"I didn't, fortunately."

"You've walked a long way from Wiltshire."

"I have. Took it easy, mind you."

"Did you get work on your way up?"

"Day labouring; anything I could get."

"What was it like?"

"Not good. Pay was poor."

"Like it is here?"

"The same. Like it is over the whole country." Jack was surprised at how the conversation was going.

"I want to do something about it," said Titus.

"Really, what *could* you do about it?"

"There's going to be a meeting in Wellesbourne on February the seventh. A chap called Joseph Arch has organised it. He'll be there, at the Stag's Head."

* * *

The following Sunday, Jack was waiting for Grace and her father at the Rose and Crown in Ratley shortly before noon. They arrived on time. Jack heard a cart rattling on the cobbles outside. He went out quickly, making sure no one was about, and there she was, his Grace. They went to each other. "I missed you a lot, Annie," he whispered.

"And I missed you, Jack, more than you know," Grace's voice was unsteady. Jack held her tight.

"Excuse me, you two. I'm cold. Let's go in." There was an empty table by a bench near the fire. Guy and Grace settled down there while Jack sat at a table nearby. He found it difficult to keep his eyes off his wife, but the plan was to stay apart, so he had to do that. Guy took a clay pipe out of his pocket, filled it with tobacco and then sauntered to Jack.

"Excuse me, do you have a light?" he asked."

"No, sorry, I haven't, but there are tapers by the fire; I'll get one." Jack went to the grate, where tapers were on the mantle shelf. He took one, lit it from the fire, and went over to Guy, cupping the taper in his hand.

"Thank you, do you want to sit with us?"

"Yes, I will." It wasn't good talking to Grace and Guy this way. He glanced around, ensuring no one was close enough to hear their conversation.

"There's going to be a meeting in Wellesbourne on Wednesday, February the seventh. Titus Ingram, a man I work with, told me that Joseph Arch has arranged the meeting at The Stag's Head. There's discontent amongst many of the farm workers, and it is widespread."

"Is Titus trustworthy?"

"He is, *and* he knows Joseph Arch."

"Then we'll meet next in Wellesbourne."

"In two weeks, at The Stag's Head."

* * *

Jack felt it appropriate to take his father's spade to the meeting at Wellesbourne. He walked with it resting on his shoulder. It was somehow symbolic, carrying such a tool to the meeting, with how it represented farm workers.

It was a cold night when Jack and Titus arrived at Wellesbourne. It was crowded and impossible to get close to the Stag's Head, let alone go into it.

Many lanterns were burning, casting a dim flickering glow on the faces of the hundreds of workers assembled. The light from a nearby lantern caught the metalwork of Jack's spade, causing the reflection to flash in his eyes. He glanced at the blade and noticed the initials T S stamped into the metalwork holding the handle. Once again, he wondered what the letters stood for.

"This is too crowded," shouted a strong voice from outside the Stag's Head. "Let's go to the village green," and the crowd of men, women and children, some of whom were babes in arms, led by the local people, headed for the village green on which grew a large chestnut tree.

"That was Joe Arch who said to go to the green," Titus said. Jack bent close to Titus to hear what he said above the hubbub of noise. "I saw Joe a few months back in the Rose and Crown in Ratley. He said he's worked on farms in the Midlands and across Wales. He's appalled by the labourers' working conditions and intends to put things right."

"What do you think about that?"

"I'm with Joe Arch, all the way."

"Me too," Jack noticed the cart, driven by Ned Pritchard, one of Guy's workers. Guy was there, with Grace at his side. "Titus, I want you to come and meet two people," Jack said. He walked over to the cart. "Titus, this is my wife and father-in-law, Grace and Guy." Titus Ingram frowned, then smiled.

"I knew things weren't quite right. Pleased to meet you, Grace and Guy. But Jack, tell me more."

"We'd better get over to the green to hear what Joe says. I'll tell you later. Ned, keep the cart near The Stag's Head. We'll be back as soon as Joe has finished."

After the meeting, Joseph Arch's voice still resonated in Jack's ears. He was glad he didn't need to live a life of deception any longer. Titus Ingram jumped at the offer of work from Guy Thompson, so the horse, a sturdy beast, had to pull the cart, now with five people, back to Sherbourne.

"Titus, we'll take you back to your place at Cripps' farm tomorrow to pick your stuff up," Guy told him. "Our friend Joseph Arch did mighty well, and the support couldn't have been better."

"Thank you, Guy. I appreciate your help. When I saw Joe, he anticipated getting thirty at his meeting in The Stag's Head. What happened tonight is incredible."

"A change in working conditions is bound to come now," Guy responded. "And now, Jack, with all that support, our task to gather evidence is no longer needed."

"I'm sure you're right."

"What evidence were you gathering?" Titus asked.

"Titus, when you asked about my past, I told you a lie. I hadn't been living rough. I went to work at the Cripps place to gather evidence of the harsh working conditions to pass on to Joseph Arch."

Titus Ingram nodded knowingly.

And thus, on that evening of February the seventh, 1872, in the flickering lamplight near the chestnut tree on the village green at Wellesbourne, in Warwickshire, was formed the National Agricultural Labourers' Union. Thanks to Joseph Arch, a sigh of relief arose from over two thousand gathered farm workers, who were *'gaunt with hunger and pinched with want'*.

Chapter 27

1872-1897

The Whitefriars Workhouse.

A shop on Queens Road in the City of Coventry sold all types of curiosities unwanted by some but needed by others. It was known by the locals as Old Ma Collins' junk shop. The shop window was a bow-fronted affair with small panes of glass, some of them bullion style. In wintertime, when snow and frost were about, and dusk was nigh, the window glowed with a warmth from within, created by coals burning in a Georgian fireplace.

Ma Collins was a character who was as warm as the glow from her fireplace shining through the window. Just behind the window a deep windowsill displayed such things as a gourd, with a skin hardened by age, from, as a label said, 'A mysterious country in the south of America.' Nestled by it was 'A Peace Pipe, from the Yankton Sioux Nation. Other objects from far and wide vied for space on the crowded windowsill. Within the shop, propped against the far wall, was an ancient flintlock rifle. Some who looked through the window thought the rifle was loaded and that Ma Collins kept it handy to prevent potential thieves.

On Friday, February the ninth, 1872, a young man in a farmworker's smock, heavily soiled but intricately embroidered, called into Old Ma Collins' shop.

The man had a spade with him.

"Good morning Stuart, and how are you today?"

"Tired. I had a long walk back from Wellesbourne. This spade was in the lane near Barford." He held out the spade.

"Do you want to buy it, ma'am?"

"Not really. We have plenty of implements of that sort." Ma Collins pointed to them, leaning against the shop's back wall. Stuart Spibey looked disappointed. He was a regular visitor to the shop, bringing items to sell that he found or, Ma Collins conjectured, that he might have stolen.

"Are you short of money again?" she asked Spibey. He nodded. This was often the case. Stuart was a gardener at the Charterhouse, which paid its workers a low wage, and he spent money as fast as he earned it.

"Let me see." She took the spade off him, felt its weight, and took in the attractiveness of the grain of the ash handle. "I'll buy it for tuppence." She felt sorry for Stuart and could tell it was a good quality implement. She would lean it in the window, and it should sell quickly for fourpence.

* * *

Kenneth Johnson was living a fractured existence. He and his family lived in the Coventry Union Workhouse at the Top of Brick Kiln Lane. He had lost his job, and the first thing to go was being able to pay the rent for his house in Court Three, in Hill Top. When the landlord threatened eviction, Ken applied for admission to the workhouse rather than his family being on the street. It meant separation for himself and his wife, but at least the children would be safe and with their mother.

The workhouse was in what was once a Carmelite monastery, the order of monks who wore white habits, hence the name Whitefriars Monastery. Ken Johnson, before the eviction, had been scrupulously honest, but not now. Now he was in a desperate fight for his family's survival. He would do anything to help them, short of physically harming people.

He sometimes obtained permission to leave the workhouse to find work. A rule that had to be obeyed before anyone left the premises was to change out of the workhouse uniform and back into their own clothes. Failure to do that would bring an accusation of theft of the uniform, followed by discharge from the workhouse and life on the street.

Ken was incensed at the situation imposed on his wife and children. It wasn't his fault he lost his job. The introduction of machinery was the problem. Mechanised looms had been introduced, and he had been the last hand weaver in the factory.

He was out once more, walking the streets looking for work. It was frosty, and there had been a heavy snowfall. When he walked into Queens Road from Greyfriars Green. The sky was yellowish, and people at home had begun to light their gas lamps.

Ken reached Old Ma Collins' place. Candles illuminated the room behind the bow window, where snow was gathering on the wooden frames. Inside, it looked warm and inviting. He stood by the window, gazing in. A woman who looked to be in her early sixties was sitting at the counter, reading. She looked up at him. Saw him shivering and signalled for him to come in. He saw her lips moving but couldn't understand that she said *Come and get warm by the fire.* However, Ken responded to the wave of her hand and went into the shop.

"Go to the fire and get warm," Ma Collins said, feeling the chill from the open door flood into the room.

"Thank you, it's turning bitter out there," he said, stooping by the fire. He held his hands close to the flames.

"What's your name?"

"Kenneth Johnson . . . Ken."

"Ken, why aren't you wearing a coat?"

"I don't have one."

"You don't have a coat in this weather?" Ma Collins, Flo to those acquainted with her, looked at the man's face. There was a kindly look about it. In her youth, she could have fallen for him. She put her book, A Tale of Two Cities, down and went to a wardrobe in the back room. She fished around in it and returned with a coat.

"Do you live around here?" she asked.

"I live near here," he said. He didn't want to say he lived in the workhouse.

"Try this on."

"But I have no money on me."

"No matter, try it." So he did, and it fitted perfectly.

"There we are. It's yours."

"But why, why give me this?" The coat was dated, probably one from several years ago, but it was in good condition, and it was thick and warm.

Flo Collins knew most people who passed by her shop and lived locally, and she was respected in the community.

"I want to give it to you because you are cold."

Ken looked at her and could tell she was genuinely interested in him. He explained,

"I lost my job, and I'm in the workhouse. My family is at one end, and I'm at the other."

"Ah, the workhouse. With your family, you say?"

Ken felt that time was pressing. "Excuse me, Mrs Collins, I have to go. I'm trying to find work." He headed for the door. "As soon as I can, I'll pay you for the coat." He went out of the shop, felt the chill as the snow flurried around him, and put his hands in the pockets of his new coat.

"Hello." A shout came from behind. He turned and saw Mrs Collins waving him back. He went back into the shop.

Florence Collins had thought quickly. She was an independent woman. She valued her independence more than most things in her life, but she did find certain things difficult these days.

Her shop occupied two of the rooms on the ground floor. The premises had a second floor and attic rooms. Maintenance work needed doing. To have a man about the house would be helpful. She had lost the love of her life in her twenties, just before they were to get married, and she determined not to marry anyone else.

"Would you like to work for me?"

Ken Johnson didn't know how to respond.

"I need someone to help me maintain the house, the shop and the garden. It's a big place, and I'm not as agile as I used to be. Finding things a bit difficult these days. There are rooms upstairs where you could live."

"But my wife and children, what would they do?"

"Can your wife cook and do laundry? I need help with those things as well."

"She's an excellent cook, and she can bake too."

"And your children?"

"Two of them, a boy, Bernard, we call him Bernie, he's seven, and we have a girl too, Claire, she's six."

Flo Collins sometimes heard the joyful sound of children nearby, and when she did, particularly in recent years, she wished she'd had children of her own.

"Bernie and Claire will be *very* welcome. And, of course, your wife is welcome too. What's her name?"

"Elaine."

"That's a nice name."

"It is. Elaine's a lovely girl. Her name is from The Lady of Shallot, by Tennyson."

"You like poetry?"

"I do."

"Then we are off to a good start. Now go and leave that workhouse place. I'll go upstairs and light the fire in your sitting room."

"I am sorry to ask, but how will we buy food and other things?"

"Would fourteen shillings a week be alright?"

"Why yes, but of course."

"Then bring your family here without further delay."

When the young man left, Flo Collins took her recent purchase, the spade she bought off Stuart Spibey, into her storage room at the back of the shop. She lovingly patted its handle. She had felt so lonely over the years and more so recently, but now things would be different.

It was unusual for inmates of the workhouse who went looking for work to return with a job. So when Ken Johnson returned with a spring in his step and asked the overseer to tell his wife and children they were leaving, the overseer asked him to repeat what he said.

Ten minutes later, Elaine and the two children entered the overseer's office. She looked pale and concerned and wondered what had happened. She couldn't understand why Ken was smiling. "What's wrong—?"

"—Nothing's wrong. We're getting out of here . . . now."

"But—"

"We've got work *and* a place to live."

"Really?"

"Really. Come on, Ellie." He held out his hands to his wife and children. Bernie and Claire ran to his arms. Ellie was a bit slower but squealed with delight and ran to him. "Mr Simms," said Ken, "Thanks for your help while we've been here, but get our belongings, please."

* * *

The snow had settled and was a few inches deep. Ken and Elaine walked arm-in-arm, smiling, although the late afternoon was bitterly cold. She told him she liked his coat. Bernie and Claire were running, sliding, slipping and falling into the softness, and throwing snowballs. Others were out, children with sledges, grown-ups enjoying the cold beauty, and others were hurrying home to get warm.

"Are we really out of there, Ken?" asked Elaine.

"Yes, we are, sweetheart. This is the start of a new life." They reached the door of Old Ma Collins' shop, "And we can be together, not you and the children at one end of the building, and me at the other. Here we are."

Ellie stepped forward to the bow window, gazed in, and saw the elderly woman sitting there, her grey hair tied in a bun, her face lit by the flickering fire. Flo Collins looked up and saw the family looking in the window. She recognised Kenneth's face and waved them in.

"Oh, how welcome you are. Come in. Close the door. Come in and get warm, my dears." Since Ken left and returned with his wife and children, Flo Collins imagined herself with a family, a son, a daughter, and two grandchildren.

* * *

The harsh winter of 1872 passed. Over the winter months, Ken repaired the wear and tear of the house. Now spring had arrived.

Flo Collins looked out of her living room at the garden. It had suffered years of neglect. She had been able to keep her shop and the room where she stored surplus goods up to scratch, but in recent years, maintaining the garden had been beyond her ability. And now, there was an ornamental border in which Ken had planted colourful shrubs, some woodbine he had found in a recent woodland walk, a Rosa Mundi, and a Jacobite rose. In addition, the old apple tree had been pruned and was coming into leaf.

Flo knocked on the window. Ken looked up, she waved, and he waved back. How peaceful things are now, she thought. But so difficult to even walk about. Elaine was doing well in the shop; she had a good way with customers. And the children were doing well at Miss Flynn's, a small school on the corner, down the road.

Time moved on, and significant changes were afoot. Electrical lighting was installed by Joseph Swan at Cragside House in Northumberland. Swan illuminated Mosley Street, in Newcastle, by electricity. Internal combustion engines were gaining popularity, and in 1896 Harry John Lawson purchased a disused four-storey cotton mill in Coventry. It became the first Horseless Carriage factory in Britain and was named Daimler. In 1897 the first Daimler motor car left the factory, and the production was three cars per week.

Chapter 28

1897-1904

Why Should We Be Ignored?

Florence Collins, Old Ma Collins died just over eight years after Ken and his family moved into her house. Her last years were the happiest of her life because the young family appreciated her generosity. Due to their seemingly boundless energy, their work repaid her more than ever she expected.

In her last will and testament, Flo left her property on Queen's Road and a sizeable amount of money to Kenneth and Elaine. A further provision was made for the children. When each of them reached the age of twenty-one, two hundred and fifty pounds held in trust for each of them was released. The years passed slowly and graciously for the family living in the property financed by items sold in the shop behind the bow window.

Bernard Johnson regularly walked out with a girl who lived near St. Thomas' church at the end of Queens Road.

It was a family type of arrangement because Bernie's sister, Claire, liked the brother of the girl Bernie was going out with. On Sunday afternoons, the two couples could be seen walking out together.

But Claire's interests were unusual for a woman of her time. She had a perfect figure, but to keep herself in that shape, she occasionally wore a plain, loose-fitting skirt and flat shoes and walked quickly around the pathways of the nearby Greyfriars Green. Sometimes she even ran, which raised the cheers and jeers of passers-by.

"Shame . . . shame to see a lady exercising in public," shouted one of them. But Claire had the strength of character to take no notice of such comments. Certain things brought out her fighting spirit. On one occasion, when a man leapt from behind a tree and tried to accost her, she punched him on the nose, which bled profusely. A Coventry Herald newspaper reporter saw the event from the park's far side. The event made bold, front-page headlines in the next edition of the Herald.

'Brave Coventry Woman.
Local teacher Claire Johnson knocked attacker, Lee Snape, to the ground, and his arrest followed.'

* * *

The ground floor of the shop, still known affectionately as 'Old Ma Collins', was now lit by electricity at the flick of a switch. After dark one September night in 1899, while the family ate, they chatted about the day's events. Ken had forgotten to light the two large candles he used to illuminate the shop atmospherically rather than using the electric bulb, which he thought was too bright.

A faint scuffling noise came from the direction of the shop, which was the other side of a stout Georgian door. Immediately but quietly, Claire stood up, placed her finger to her lips and, moving swiftly to the door, grasped the handle. Bernie stood next, just as quiet but slower than Claire. He tried to force his way in front of her to open the door, but she resisted. Then she wrenched open the door and immediately switched on the light. Two men were in the room, each holding some valuable silverware put aside for auction.

Ken and Elaine came to the doorway, shouting at the intruders, and they saw Claire in action. She grasped the old flintlock rifle, a remnant of Flo Collins' days, by the barrel and swung it in an arc. The butt hit the taller intruder, who shouted in pain. The silverware clattered to the floor, and the two men fled from the shop.

As Claire hastened to the shop door, her father tried to hold onto her sleeve to stop her, but she shook herself free. She stepped outside. "And don't you come back," she shouted. "Next time, this gun will be loaded." She looked at it and noticed a slight bend in the barrel that hadn't been there before.

* * *

The year 1900 arrived. What celebrations there were! Victoria Regina had been Queen and Empress for sixty-four years, and now there was the dawn of a new century. Astounding changes had been wrought in the eighteen hundreds. Great steamships plied the Atlantic, some reaching speeds of over twenty knots. It seemed the whole world was being powered by steam and lit by gas. But electricity was coming more into public awareness as a source of power.

Ken and Elaine had reached the age of fifty-five and were finding time for relaxation in their garden. They loved the peace and the birdsong. The spade Flo Collins gave him all those years ago was an object of affection for Ken, and he only used it to edge the lawn. Afterwards, he would clean it thoroughly. Then he would hang it in the summerhouse as one might hang a picture on a wall.

When Bernie Johnson, their son, was fourteen years old, he began working for an auctioneer, initially as a general labourer. He progressed well, and when he was nineteen, the auction house owner in Jesson Street gave Bernie a new gavel. So at nine o'clock one Wednesday morning Bernard Johnson grasped the gavel confidently and conducted his first auction. In time, when the owner decided to work fewer hours, Bernie became the manager of the auction house.

Bernie's sister, Claire, had grown to adulthood with a spiky nature and a tendency to be forthright and opinionated. Ken privately told Elaine that he thought Claire was a *Bit of a Firebrand*. This part of her character sometimes broke loose when they were around the dinner table. The conversation was occasionally about Coventry's rapid industrial expansion. It was an exciting time of change. New factories were being built, and old factories and mills were being converted for the new industries.

The City had expanded over the past two decades. Rows of terraced houses were being built on the City's outskirts. Instead of being isolated villages, Earlsdon, Coundon, and Foleshill became part of an industrial conglomerate. Top Shops built above some dwellings enabled tradespeople and their families to live and work at home. The growth of mechanised industry attracted labour to Coventry from all over the British Isles and from overseas.

"The problem is that there is no equality in those factories," Claire said. "The women workers are paid far less than the men, but often they do equal work. We don't even have the vote to put any of this right." Claire was wearing a white blouse with a high collar, which showed her rising colour. The situation angered her.

"That's all very well, Claire," Elaine stepped in, "But what can be done about it? As you say, men hold sway in parliament too." Then, to reassure Kenneth, Elaine added, "You aren't like that, Ken, but many men are. Male dominance is entrenched in the owners of many factories. It's the way some of those places have been run for what, a hundred and fifty years?"

"At least. But it won't be like that for much longer," said Claire.

"What do you mean?" asked Ken.

"Have you heard of Ida Slater?"

"Isn't she one of the Suffragettes?" he asked.

"She is—"

"—I met her recently," interjected Elaine.

"Did you really, whereabouts did you meet her?"

"In the Gulson Library. She came and sat next to me. We started chatting."

Claire wanted to know more.

"She was looking into some of the writings of John Stuart Mill. He wrote an essay entitled The Subjection of Women. Ida said she often goes to the library."

Claire was impressed by her mother. She wanted to meet Ida Slater, so mother and daughter started to walk to the Gulson Reference Library each day. A new facet of Elaine Johnson's personality was revealed to her daughter. During these times they had together, they chatted openly about the standing of women in society. Claire was surprised by how strongly her mother felt about the unfair situation.

"If you had the opportunity to do something about it, what would you choose to do?" asked Claire one day as they neared the library.

"What can we do?"

"We need to make an impression, a statement about how we feel." As she said that, Claire's voice took on a stern tone. Elaine hadn't heard this in her daughter before. She knew Claire was, as Ken said, a while back, *a Firebrand*, and by her action when the robbery took place in the shop, it was obvious that Claire could be formidable. The historical character of Joan of Arc sometimes came into Elaine's mind when she tried to fathom the depths of her daughter's personality.

During their first meeting, Ida Slater immediately took to Claire and Elaine. First, they talked about their interest in local history, and then, the subject changed to the rights of women.

"I have a problem with John Stuart Mill's assertions," Ida said. "He stated that he wouldn't include the uneducated having the right to vote. I maintain that, if they want to, everyone should be allowed to vote, whatever their social standing or level of education. And Mill was too philosophical about those he thought would be eligible to vote."

"True. One doesn't have to be educated to decide who would be a good Member of Parliament. But at least, as a Member of Parliament, Mill did demand the right of women to vote, so that was a start for us," said Claire. "But definitely, the vote should be for everyone."

"It should. Listen," Ida drew close so she wouldn't be overheard. "I have a suggestion for you both. I'm going to

London next week to meet with the Pankhursts. Would you like to come with me?" she asked.

"I certainly would," Claire's response was immediate. "I'm impressed by the Pankhursts. Given time, and if we can drum up support, we'll achieve what we need."

The train pulled into Coventry Station. Claire was always impressed when she saw the mighty steam engines painted, polished and gleaming. In a sense, they were alive. So a shiver went down her back when one of them, heading for Birmingham, towing a dozen or more carriages, raced through the station full-tilt, its massive connecting rods just a blur to the eye. And then their train came in, and Claire and Ida climbed on board.

Elaine had gone to the station to wave Claire off. She was apprehensive because Claire's character was unpredictable, and Elaine wondered what would come next after she met the Pankhursts.

The guard blew his whistle, and when he waved a green flag, the engine's whistle shrieked, and the London-bound train began to move.

Chapter 29

1904-1910

Into The Edwardian Age

In 1904 the old Queen died, and the Edwardian age began. Just a year before, in 1903, near Kitty Hawk, in North Carolina, Orville and Wilbur Wright took off in the Wright Flyer, and the aviation age began.

Some called the time of Edward the Seventh *The Golden Age*. So it was for a little while, with the achievements that were accomplished and the pleasant peace that appeared to reign for the first few years of the twentieth century. But all that was apparent on the surface disguised what else was happening. The traits of greed and acquisition demonstrated by governments holding tight onto the reins of national power and wanting even more power created a deadly undercurrent ready to gush forth.

Events did not go well for the Suffragettes. For several years their attempts to achieve recognition were limited to Parliamentary procedure, but this had little effect. As a result of the strident voices speaking out, it became apparent that there was great unhappiness with the lack of equality for women. Despite this, most men in power denied women's need for change.

Hopes were raised in 1906 when most Members of Parliament agreed on the need for equality. But the hopes were dashed after two years at the time of another election. This continuous cycle of hope and despair brought the need for more decisive action. The Suffragettes were determined women who possessed great courage. They were prepared to face mortal danger by becoming militant to achieve equality and the right to vote.

After dark one summer day in 1909, Claire Johnson took a bag into the garden at the back of the shop on Queens Road. She picked up two fist-size lumps of Warwickshire Sandstone and put those, a three-inch paintbrush and a jar of paste she made out of flour, into her bag. Then, she made her way into the town, using narrow, dark side streets and keeping close to the buildings.

Claire reached Bailey Lane. Keeping in the darkness away from the street light, she made her way to St. Mary's Guildhall, the medieval building where Coventry City Council met. Claire put down her bag gently so as not to make any noise, took the *Votes for Women* banner from her bag and pasted it onto the sizeable Gothic entry doors of the Guildhall. Now, the noise didn't matter. She took the stones from her bag, moved down the street a few yards, kept shouting "Votes for women" as loud as she could and hurled the stones at two old stained glass windows.

Only seconds later, Claire heard shouts, a whistle and then heavy footsteps running in her direction. She stayed where she was, undaunted by the approaching threat. Then two burly policemen came around the corner, grasped her roughly and handcuffed her.

The court session was held in the room where Claire smashed the stained glass windows. As she came up the stairs from the cell, Claire saw boards placed temporarily over the windows. "That gives you something to think about," she shouted at the judge.

"Silence in court," shouted the court usher in response.

"Miss Johnson, if you carry on like that, you will be held in contempt of court," announced Judge Henry Wallace.

"There will be two more smashed tonight," shouted a man from the public gallery. Claire scanned the crowded gallery and saw her long-standing fiancé.

"Who was that?" Shouted the judge. There was silence. "Have a policeman stand in the public gallery." A police sergeant left the courtroom and shortly appeared upstairs in the gallery. "If there is more disturbance in this court, that person will be arrested for disturbing the peace. Now, let us proceed."

The trial lasted a bare twenty minutes, at the end of which Claire was sentenced. "We cannot allow such behaviour to take place. It is against the common good. Therefore I sentence you to twelve months imprisonment in Holloway. You will be transferred there forthwith."

Her mother, in the public gallery, was proud of her daughter. "Be brave, my darling," she called as Claire was led back down to the cells. Claire looked up and smiled. Ida Slater, usually relaxed but now grim-faced, waved to Claire. Not a cheery wave but a sincere wave of acknowledgement.

The clothes handed to the women incarcerated in Holloway were intended to make them feel demeaned. All the clothes had an arrow on them. They were given red striped stockings, but nothing was given to hold them up. Inmates were given a badge showing their cell and cell block number. Throughout her imprisonment, each woman was known by that cell number, not her name. Claire Johnson was number 36C.

Three months into her sentence, Claire and a number of the other Suffragettes went on a hunger strike to make the authorities take them seriously. Those in authority decided to force-feed them. So when they approached Claire with the tube, two warders and a doctor got considerably more than they bargained for, ending up bloodied. But a group of warders overpowered her, and the humiliation and the pain began.

After twelve months, number 36C's sentence finished. It was 1910 when Claire breathed the air of freedom outside Holloway. Things had changed within the movement that she was not prepared to accept. Smashing windows was one thing. Using bombs was another. Total militancy was planned, and nitro-glycerine was to be the agent. *There must be a different way of gaining equality rather than endangering life,"* Claire thought. But the achievement of equality was helped by a method that plumbed humanity's darkest depths.

When she stepped off the train, Kenneth and Elaine Johnson welcomed Claire with kisses and tears. It was August the twelfth, 1910, the year Ken and Ellie reached the age of sixty-five. Bernie had married his fiancé earlier that year. So until later that day, when he and his wife would come for a family reunion meal, Claire sat with her parents in the living room. They listened to their daughter's experiences in Holloway, and Ken was incensed at the treatment meted out to their daughter. Elaine sat there, pale and quiet, a handkerchief to her face.

"I've finished with it, Mum. With the Suffragettes." She explained the threats of violence the women were planning. "I don't intend to harm anyone. I agree with the principle of equality, but there has to be another way of dealing with the matter."

"I do agree with you," said her mother. "And I'm glad you're stepping back."

"I am, too," said her father. "I tell you what, if I got hold of whoever did those things to you, I would skin them alive." Kenneth stood. He was shaking with anger.

"Come on, Dad. Come and sit down. It's done now. It's in the past." Claire patted the seat, and Ken, breathing quick and deeply, sat back down. Shortly afterwards, Bernie and Molly arrived, and the evening was a happy and memorable occasion.

The shop in Queens Road had done well financially, and when the auction house in Jesson Street came up for sale, Kenneth could purchase it. It was a natural progression that a shop buying and selling all manner of second-hand goods, some of them antique and very valuable, would branch into auctioneering. Bernie ran the business. He had a strong voice and a natural flair when standing at the rostrum with a gavel. Some people attended the auction each Wednesday because they found Bernie's jocular manner entertaining.

Like his predecessor, Florence Collins, Kenneth whiled away the time between customers by reading novels. Behind the shop counter, near the back wall, his chair faced the window and the road outside. The street was busy when people were going to or from work. Some walked, many had pedal cycles, others rode motorcycles, and just the odd few had motor carriages, cars, as the vehicles were called.

Some of these vehicles were tall and unattractive, like a post-chaise without the horses. But one car in particular that went by the shop morning and evening was different. It was a low vehicle, and it was long. Ken began to go out of the shop to look at the car when he expected it to pass by. The driver started to give him a wave, and one day he stopped the car outside the shop.

"Like to come for a ride?" The man shouted above the noise of the engine. Ken nodded. The driver stepped out, came to the passenger door and opened it. Ken climbed in and sat on a luxurious leather seat.

The driver introduced himself as Barnabas Hennessey.

"Call me Barney," he said as he grasped a long lever with a knob on top and moved it forward, at which the car began to travel along with an impressive growling noise. Ken was smitten.

"It's a twenty-horse-power Beeston Humber," the individual said in a broad Birmingham accent. "Got it a few months back from the factory in Nottingham. They've opened a new factory in Stoke, just round the corner."

"I know the place. Been to a house near the factory to collect some furniture for auction." Barney moved the long lever again, pulling it toward him.

What is that?" Ken asked.

"The gearstick."

"What's it for?"

"To change how fast you can go. If you go up an incline, you go into a low gear because it's got more power. You use top, the fourth gear along the straight and level."

"What do you think of Daimler vehicles? Ken asked.

"They're OK. But I prefer the Beeston Humber's design."

* * *

"They're dangerous things," Elaine advised him. She had seen the car Ken had a ride in and had taken an instant dislike to it. It was so different to a coach, not so gentle, and there were no horses. Her hearing was failing, and she thought he had called it a Beast of a Humber.

"No," he raised his voice. "It's a Beeston Humber. Beeston's in Nottingham. It's where those cars are built."

After some months and several practice sessions driving Barney's car, Kenneth, against the wishes of Elaine, bought a Beeston Humber. Three days after its delivery, and after more practice locally, Ken proposed to Elaine that they have a trip to Royal Leamington Spa.

"Our car gives us a lot more freedom. We can take the road through Kenilworth and go to Jephson Gardens in Leamington. There's a restaurant where we can have a meal."

Against her better judgment, Elaine acquiesced and, wearing her best summer dress, she was helped into the passenger seat by Claire, who was about to walk to the school where she worked.

"Have a nice day," she called and waved as the car moved off. She was going to accompany her parents to Leamington, but one of the other teachers was ill, and Claire was asked to cover for her.

Jephson Gardens was just as Elaine remembered when she was taken there as a child. An addition since she went last was a restaurant next to the tropical glasshouse. It was humid inside the glasshouse, and they enjoyed an ice cream soda with their meal. Afterwards, they went to the

Pump-rooms, sampled the spa water, and then walked up The Parade. It had been a thoroughly enjoyable day.

"I want to start going back home while there's plenty of daylight left," Kenneth said as they walked back down The Parade past the statue of Queen Victoria, holding the Orb and Sceptre.

Ken decided to take a different route back home, going through Lillington and Stoneleigh Village rather than Kenilworth. "It's a scenic route. It goes by the grounds of Stoneleigh Abbey," Ken said as he cranked the starting handle. After several turns, the engine fired up with its pleasing growl, attracting some onlookers.

They made steady progress; Ken wasn't a fast driver. He was content to drive steadily to take in the surroundings. The gentle speed was soothing to Elaine, who went over the lovely day in her mind. She liked the Beeston Humber now.

"That was a lovely day, Ken. We must do it again." He was pleased with what she said. It made the future look bright and promising.

"I love you, Ellie," he said, touching her hand as they came to a bend in the road. A sign at the side of the road said *Steep Hill,* and there was a black triangle on the road sign.

"I've heard that some have cycled up this hill," Ken said as they approached its brow. Elaine held the side of her seat. The road seemed to drop away in front of them. She glanced down and saw the village of Stoneleigh way down to her left, nestled into the side of the River Sowe. Then, further along the river, she saw where it merged with the Avon.

The car started to gain speed as Ken negotiated his way down the hill. He applied the brake, but nothing happened. His heart missed a beat. "Something's wrong," he said.

"What?"

"It's the brakes. They're not working." He tried to keep a straight course as they gathered speed. He attempted to change into a low gear, but all that happened was a harsh grating noise.

"Oh, Ken," Elaine said as she glanced at the roadside racing by. She saw a dial on the dashboard with a pointer touching the figure, 60. She glanced up. A road crossed their path at the bottom of the hill, and a steam roller, belching smoke and steam, suddenly appeared from behind some trees. They were racing nearer and nearer, the steam roller uttered a piercing whistle and then . . .

Chapter 30

1910-1914

A Time of Change

The funeral of Kenneth and Elaine Johnson took place at St Thomas's Church, which was just down the road from where Ken and Ellie lived. Bernie, usually quite stoic in his approach to life, was trying to deal with the grief.

Friends and relatives, and some strangers, attended the funeral. Kenneth had been popular in local society. He had sometimes taken the rostrum at an auction sale under the expert guidance of his son. And the story of the family's rags to riches life, into the workhouse and then out of it one snowy afternoon, had struck a chord with local people.

Molly, Bernard Johnson's wife, took care of the arrangements. She organised food and drink at the family home after the service. The items from the shop were at the auction house, ready for sale, and people chatted quietly in the house and the garden.

After the funeral, Barnabas Hennessey slipped into Ken's summerhouse, trying to escape the other people. He looked around the room, a place of relaxation with a settee and armchairs. A table had a tray with cups and saucers, things of everyday living. But another item hanging on the wall was out of character. It was a spade with a wooden handle and a distinctive grain. It was like a work of art hanging on the wall. Barney approached it. The blade was polished and slightly concave, distorting his reflection. Two letters were stamped on the socket, a *T* and an *S*.

Barney was trying to come to terms with introducing the Beeston Humber to Ken, in which he and Elaine were killed. He knew their death was a random accident, Ken and Elaine being in the wrong place at the wrong time. But Barney had become good friends with Ken. The accident would never have happened if he had carried on waving instead of stopping to see if Ken wanted a ride.

Soon after the accident, Barney sold his Beeston Humber and bought a Daimler. He wouldn't have bought another car if he didn't need to travel for his work. He was unsettled and sat down in one of the armchairs.

Claire wanted time to herself. So as people were gathered indoors, eating sandwiches, drinking tea or, by choice, sherry, she went into the garden. The sky was overcast, with thick black clouds on the horizon, which seemed appropriate for the day of the funeral. Lightning flashed from one of the clouds; A few seconds later, there was a distant peal of thunder, and Claire reached the summerhouse door just as heavy rain began to fall.

Barnabas Hennessey was in one of the armchairs, writing in a notebook. He looked pale and drawn. He raised his hand as she came in.

"Hello, Claire," he said, raising his hand.

"Barney, how are you?"

"More to the point, how are you?"

"Oh, trying to get used to things . . . to the emptiness of life now."

Claire went to the other armchair, sat down and wiped away the tears. "I should have been in that car with them."

"No, you shouldn't. Don't say that."

"Barney, I was meant to be with them."

"What do you mean?" he frowned.

"I was going with them to Leamington. The day before, I was told I was needed in school, so I didn't go. I should have been in that car."

"You mustn't feel bad about that. Your Mum and Dad wouldn't want you to. They would be glad you weren't in it."

"I suppose they would."

"And we aren't in control of circumstances that sometimes occur. They are out of our control. But, listen, Claire, I have a problem I must overcome too."

"And what's that?"

Barney told Clair about stopping the car and asking Ken if he would like to go for a ride. This familiar guilt feeling between them brought Claire and Barney close, at first as advisors, a hearing ear during stressful times. But then they realised that the relationship was deeper than that, to the extent that they felt complete together. They were married in September of 1911, and by August 1912, Claire gave birth to a son they called Lester.

A few weeks after Lester's birth, Claire and her brother sold the property on Queens Road. The house and garden were cleared, and everything was sold at auction.

May of 1910 brought sadness to Great Britain because it was the year King Edward the Seventh died. His son was crowned King George the Fifth just over a year later. In Europe, nations were aligning themselves. Some of the countries were vying for power and had the urge to expand their borders. Other countries were sure they would keep hold of territories acquired in the past by force of arms.

Consequently, alliances were made that forged groups of nations into polar opposites. On the one hand, there was the Triple Entente, consisting of the Russian Empire, the French Third Republic and the United Kingdom of Great Britain and Northern Ireland. On the other hand, there was the Triple Alliance, Germany, the Austro-Hungarian Empire and Italy.

Over the previous few years, there had been skirmishes and wars related to the major European powers. The continent of Europe, its nations and dependences stretched to the world's width, resembled a simmering cauldron. The rumblings on the continent that Barney heard of from his brother, who taught English in Verdun, were worrying.

Claire and Barney's son was nearly two years old when an event lit a mighty fuse. In Sarajevo, on June 28, 1914, Austrian Archduke Franz Ferdinand and his wife were assassinated. The cauldron had reached boiling point, fires were lit worldwide, and the pot boiled over.

Chapter 31

1914-1919

A generation Sacrificed

Greed and acquisition.

We want that land. Damn you, we will enter your borders. Our power is absolute, and peace will never be an option.

Times were disruptive and challenging. *'Your Country Needs You,'* the poster of Lord Kitchener, in public places, invited a generation of young men to the potential battlefields of Europe. With war looming, lads from all over the land, and the Empire, lent their lives to England and began military training.

And then, finally, war was declared, and the lads were crowding the stations, bound for Europe, smiling, waving.

"See you soon, Ma."

"Bye Johnny . . . you'll soon be nineteen. I'll bake you a cake when you get back home."

They looked so smart in their uniforms as they waited for transport to take them to where the bullets flew.

23rd August 1914

The fire on the altar of sacrifice for the British Expeditionary Force was lit at Mons. Trenches were dug for shelter from the bullets. The headlines in the press told of bravery amidst the horrors the boys had been urged to face.

And then Johnny and Hans lay dying.

* * *

Since the war started, the price of goods in the shops had increased so much that Alec Webster and his wife, Sadie, decided they had to do something about it. It wasn't that they were in debt. They managed to get a mortgage and pay their way, but they had to be careful. Alec and Sadie bought as much as they could second-hand or at auction to save money if they needed anything for the house.

Alec, who was twenty-five, had a job at Alfred Herbert's factory in Upper York Street, where he had served his apprenticeship. He worked as a machine tester, a reserved occupation, under Frank Bates, the foreman of the test bay. Sadie, just a few months younger than Alec, was a cook in the canteen at the same factory.

They had been at the house in Moor Street for a year and were still trying to make the home their own rather than containing shadows of the previous owner. They were making progress. Then the war began, and their plans were shelved.

Due to the short supply of foodstuffs in the local shops, Alec and Sadie decided to dig up the back lawn and use the land for growing food.

"Maybe the war won't last long," Sadie said, hoping her words held true. Alec went into his garden shed. A few weeks after moving into Moor Street, he and Sadie went to the auction rooms in Jesson Street. Lot 62 was a job lot of garden tools, amongst which was a wheelbarrow and a small lawn mower. He bid for them successfully. He used the lawn mower each Sunday in the growing season and a hoe and a rake to keep the borders weed-free.

"Shall we dig it all, Sadie, to grow our food?" he called.

"I think so. The more we dig, the better for the time being. Then, we can re-seed the lawn at some point."

"Right you are. Here goes." Alec thrust the spade at the lawn and put his weight on it. "I'm glad this spade's sharp," he said, rubbing his hand on the smooth handle.

Digging the vegetable bed took him four sessions over four Sundays. Then, when the last row was dug, he straightened up and rubbed his back. "Ready to plant the spuds," he said. "Just need to rake it."

"We can put fruit bushes in the border here," called Sadie, who was lightening the soil with a fork in one of the borders. "And we can plant raspberries along the fence."

They walked into the town to Rider Betts and bought some seed potatoes. Then, they shared the weight of the carrier bag on the way home, a handle apiece. When they reached the start of Albany Road, they heard the sound of rapid gunfire in the distance.

"Now, what do we do?" asked Sadie. She sounded nervous. Alec looked into the sky where, in the distance, he could hear a peculiar droning noise, and he saw a long, silver cigar-shaped object in the direction of Whitley.

"It's one of those Zeppelins," he pointed.

"What are those things around it?" Sadie asked.

Alec squinted, put his hand up to shield his eyes from the Sun and saw what Sadie was on about. Three small black silhouettes were circling the Zeppelin. He recognised the distinctive bi-plane wings.

"They're Sopwith Camels. They've taken off from Whitley airfield." Alec was excited. "Come on, lads, get him," he shouted, and they heard the distant sound of machine guns again. The noise didn't last long. A sudden flash of flame erupted from the airship's side and travelled quickly along its length. It broke in two and then disappeared from view.

The day after the event, information was headlined in the local press that businesses and households should take very seriously the need to;

Dim Your Lights Whenever Possible at night,
in case of air raids by the evil Hun.

Our gallant Royal Flying Corps lads in their Sopwith Camels knocked a Zeppelin for six over Whitley Common's cricket pitch. The wreckage lies there for all to see. Be aware that the evil Hun may see you from above. Buy candles in case your lights need to be extinguished!

———————

As the fires intensified in Europe, it seemed at times that there was an air of celebration. On one occasion, the Royal Warwickshire Volunteer Regiment band led the Warwick's through the streets of Coventry, led by Armourer Staff Sergeant George Horton, playing the piccolo. Then, the Warwicks left for Weymouth on a train with the flag of the Union fixed to the front. As the train left, the band finished the stirring march they were playing and began the cadences of Auld Lang Syne.

Groups of men left factories destined for a different type of work, and those who remained worked long hours to satisfy the need for war equipment. The Suffragette movement suspended militancy. Women were asked to work in factories and were welcomed with open arms. How the need for women's involvement in production altered in times of national emergency!

And priests on both sides of the battle lines prayed over the lads before facing each other in France and Belgium's fields, where the bullets were flying.

Almost two thousand years previously, the Messiah spoke these words that would identify his true followers, who would be lovers of peace, whatever the cost to themselves;

I am giving you a new commandment, that you love one another; just as I have loved you, you also love one another.

By this all will know that you are my disciples—if you have love among yourselves."

Did the priests tell the lads to lay down their arms?

Johnny and Hans lay dead, sacrificed on the altar of war.

"Goodbye, Ma."

"Goodbye Johnny, you would've been nineteen. I was going to bake you a cake, Johnny, my lovely son, but I won't be doing that now."

* * *

The long and deadly four years ended on 11th November 1918. In Saint-Denis, six miles from Paris, men gathered in a railway carriage with pens rather than guns and signed the Armistice.

What celebrations were at the end of the War to End All Wars! The Royal Warwickshire Volunteer Regiment's band led the Warwicks through Coventry town again. Armourer Staff Sergeant George Horton was in the lead with his piccolo. After the march through the town, George arrived at his home on Marlborough Road.

"Who's that man?" George's youngest son, Doug, asked his mother. "It's your father," she told him. "He's been away at war in Europe."

When Doug was older, his father showed him a fountain pen. "Bet you don't know where I got this pen," George said.

"Where was it, Dad, WH Smith's?"

"There lies a story. I found this pen in the Sinai Desert while working for the Sharif of Mecca."

"What were you doing there?"

"Well, you know I'm an Armourer Staff Sergeant," his son nodded, "The Arab's rifles were old and decorative. They were shiny and reflected the sunlight, giving away their position to the enemy. We had a pickling vat, and we dulled the guns down with a liquid we call gun blue."

* * *

"Shall we lay the lawn again, Sadie?" asked Alec one evening while they were playing cards near the fire.

"That's a good idea. We will have a lawn again, but we should make the lawn smaller and keep some of the vegetable bed."

"OK. Maybe it could be half the size it used to be. I'll start preparing the lawn tomorrow."

Chapter 32

1919-1931

The Jazz Age and the Riddings

It was a time for relaxing. A sigh of relief arose across the world. In Great Britain, the war had demonstrated the skills that women were capable of, proving they were equally skillful and efficient as men, in some instances even better. The Parliament Act 1918 was passed that year, allowing women to be elected to Parliament. The race for Votes for Women was on.

Art and architecture were in a state of change. In a short span of years, Art Nouveau, with its soft and delicious curves, was diminishing. Now angular was the rage, with Art Deco artists and architects in a state of busy creation, taking the world by storm using pencil, paint, bricks, concrete and stone.

* * *

During the dinner breaks at Alfred Herbert Machine Tools, Alec and Frank Bates often sat together. "I've just bought a plot of land in The Riddings," Frank said.

"Whereabouts?"

"About halfway down the lane. I'm having a house built near the stream. Fancy helping me out, clearing the land?"

Work started the following Sunday. Alec wheelbarrowed some tools along, and when he arrived at Frank's place, he surveyed the plot. It was large and square, surrounded by mature trees, and had a stream at the bottom. On the other side of the stream was an extensive golf course. A greenhouse was already installed, with a rockery nearby.

"You've worked on this quickly," said Alec.

"Not really. It used to be an allotment. The greenhouse was already here, but I built the rockery."

"What do you want me to do?"

"Well, I want a pond here," Frank pointed next to the rockery. "We'll mark it out, and then we'll both do some digging. Can I use your spade?" He marked out the perimeter of the pond, making one edge six inches away from the concave outline of the rockery and the outer edge he marked into a kidney shape. The steel of the spade rang when he rubbed off the soil. "Where did you get this?"

"Bought it at auction after we moved into Moor Street."

"It's a good one. Not mass produced. The blade wasn't stamped in one hit. Look," Frank touched the front of the blade and turned it a fraction so that the reflection moved slightly. He pointed to slight irregularities stretching down the length of the blade. "It's old. Someone formed this spade on a tilt hammer."

"Never noticed that before; you've got good eyes."

"Comes with experience in the machine tool trade."

Over the following months, work progressed well on the Bates' house, and Frank, his wife, Elizabeth, who he called Liz, and their children moved in toward the end of September 1921. Their four sons and their daughter loved the place. The large garden and the sense of freedom was delicious after the smaller house where they previously lived. In addition, the Riddings was quietly secluded. The narrow road wasn't a practical shortcut, so there was little passing traffic. It was like living in the country even though large factories were within walking distance.

Sometimes, if the wind was in the right direction, Frank could hear the faint noise of machinery at the Standard Motor Company's factory at Canley. But, to Frank, that wasn't a problem. The distant sound of machinery, some of it made by Alfred Herbert, was like a lullaby, and it was healthy for the economy. After the destruction and horrors of war, life was again progressing normally.

* * *

It took the grass of Alec's new lawn, which he had rolled a few times, a while to grow long and strong enough before he could cut it. But when it reached an inch and a half, he took the mower out of the shed, oiled it and gave the grass its first cut. Alec was pleased with how the lawn looked with the familiar stripes on the grass.

Then he heard music coming from next door. He glanced furtively over the fence. The French Windows were open, and the couple who lived there were dancing closely, in a lively fashion, but not touching each other. The dance was nothing like a quickstep; it looked more like gymnastics.

The lively beat stuck in Alec's mind while he carried on cutting the lawn, and when he stopped at the end of one of the rows, he could still hear the music. Again, it was catchy but a different tune this time. He started tapping his foot and wanted to dance to the beat like the couple next door.

He put the mower's handle down, went to the kitchen door and called Sadie. "Come and listen to this," he said, grasping her hand. "Come on," and then Sadie heard the music. She peeped through a hole in the fence, saw the energetic dance, and liked what she saw.

"Shall we do it, Alec?"

"Let's have another look." He wanted to know how to do the steps. Sadie moved away from the hole and began jigging to the beat.

She stopped. "Won't be a minute," she said. She had seen how Elsie, the girl next door, was dressed. She had on one of the 'Flapper' dresses, above the knee, showing the figure.

Sadie dashed upstairs and changed into a dress she bought last week from Helena Evan's dress shop on Earlsdon Street. Sadie glanced at herself in the full-length mirror and smiled as she shimmied in front of it. "That'll do," she muttered, then dashed back to Alec and the music.

He heard her open the kitchen door and turned away from the hole in the fence. "Oh, I say . . ."

"Like it?"

"Like it? I like you in it."

"Shall we dance?" Sadie had an inbuilt sense of rhythm, and she began to dance, the same as Elsie. "Come on Alec Webster. It's the roaring twenties."

Chapter 33

Times, They Are a Changing

In 1918, men over twenty-one became entitled to vote, and women were allowed to vote if they were over thirty. However, due to the number of men killed in the Great War, more women were left in the population than men. Therefore, to preserve male dominance in Parliament, the men of the Government raised women's voting age so that fewer women than men would be entitled to vote, thus keeping women in a subservient place.

In 1928 the Representation of the People (Equal Franchise) Act 1928 was passed in Parliament. This finally brought about voting equality between men and women.

But things began to happen in The United States of America that would have a marked effect on the whole world. It was not bombs and bullets. Instead, it had to do with money, the lack of it.

The place was 18 Broad Street, Manhattan, the Wall Street Stock Exchange. Since 1928 the stock market sometimes surged. As a result, people tended to throw money into stocks to get rich quickly. However, the world of finance was unstable, and economists recommended that it would be wise to show caution with savings.

Under normal circumstances, to the casual onlooker, stock exchange activity anytime was frantic. But on Thursday, October 24th, 1929, the action was extra frantic because the market surged and suddenly dropped eleven per cent. By October the 28th, there had been widespread panic, with millions of shares sold. Thirty billion dollars worth of shares were lost the day after, and many investors were wiped out.

It didn't take long for stock exchanges worldwide to feel the ripples of the Wall Street crash. The panic quickly started to affect industry. As cash in the pocket dried up, sales of unessential products decreased. The knock-on effect was that fewer people were needed to make products in the manufacturing industries. As a result, workers were laid off, particularly in Northern England, Scotland, Wales and Northern Ireland. Exports from Britain decreased by half, and in some places, unemployment grew to seventy per cent of the workforce.

There was a significant shift in labour. As poverty became more apparent, some families in broad unemployment areas moved from where they lived to get work. Some with the energy to do so walked a long distance. One man, who had the nickname Dai Curly, walked from Top Trebanog, near Pontypridd, in Wales, to Coventry for work. A few months later, after he found work and a place to live, his family followed, and what celebrations there were.

In the areas with mass unemployment, government handouts called 'The Dole' helped those who qualified. Times were critical for those who didn't qualify. There were also those whose work situation was unaffected by the decrease in manufactured goods. During the early 1930s, the English Midlands began seeing the motor industry's seismic growth with Austin and Morris, whose factories in Coventry, Birmingham and Oxford flourished under the drive of Leonard Lord.

Chapter 34

1932-1936

Industry, and Berlin

In April of 1932, Frank Bates was due to accompany an order of Alfred Herbert's capstan lathes to Omsk and then Tomsk in Russia's Siberia. Whether the order would be cancelled was touch and go for a while. But with Russian industry trying to compete on the world stage, the order went ahead.

"How long will you be away?" Liz asked. They were near the rockery and the pond, where some goldfish were lazily basking.

Frank sprinkled some ant eggs into the pond. "I'll be away about three weeks. I wish it wasn't that long, but I'm afraid it goes with the job. Depends on how easily the installation of the machinery goes."

Liz looked troubled. "I do hope you'll be safe. Things are still uncertain over there."

"Don't worry, love. I'll make sure me and the lads keep well out of trouble." He held her tight.

Four of the Test Bay team, including Alec Webster, with Frank Bates in charge, crossed the English Channel by ferry and took the train from Ostend for the first leg of the journey to Siberia. They stopped at Berlin's Anhalter Bahnhof. From the station, a tunnel connected to the massive Excelsior Hotel on Askanischen Platz, where the engineers were to spend the night.

Frank went to his room and glanced at his pocket watch. Half past two in the afternoon. He needed to get some

German money, and, given the time, he needed to find the nearest bank quickly. He went downstairs to the foyer and saw a bar where several people with drinks were engaged in serious conversation. He decided to test his German. Three men in grey suits stood at the bar, and he approached them.

"Bitte, wo ist die nächste Bank?" Then, he noticed the armband each was wearing on the left arm. The bands were red, and they had a white circle with a black cross and a projection to the right at the end of each leg of the cross.

One of the men turned to look at him. He was of average height and build. He had black hair and a narrow, black Charlie Chaplin moustache that looked vaguely comical. But there, the humour ended. What Frank noticed were the man's eyes. They were the coldest eyes he had ever seen.

The man answered, "Es gibt eine Deutsche Bank am Alexanderplatz und eine weitere in der Straße Unter den Linden." Frank thanked him and turned to go.

But then, "Sind sie ein Auslander?" the man asked in an authoritarian tone. He had picked up Frank's foreign accent.

"Ja, ich bin ein Englander", he replied. He instantly disliked the man, feeling he couldn't trust him or the rest of the group, who had turned to look at him. They looked hard and unforgiving. He was damned if he was going to mention the real reason for his stay at the hotel, that he was en route to Russia with a machinery consignment. So he said he was on holiday touring German cultural places.

"Ich bin im Urlaub und besuche die Kunstgalerien und Museen in Berlin."

"Ja? Dann genießen Sie Ihren Aufenthalt."

He understood that the man, who appeared to be leading the group, said for him to enjoy his stay, and Frank thanked him. Just then, Alec Webster entered the bar, giving Frank the excuse to leave.

"I need to get some German money, Alec. Feel like a walk?"

"Yeah, where's the bank?"

"Alexanderplatz, hang on." Frank went to the concierge.

"Bitte, wo ist der Alexanderplatz?" The man looked at Frank, smiled and gave the directions in English.

When they got outside, Alec asked, "Who the hell was that group in the bar?"

"I'm not sure, but I'm glad you came when you did. I recognised those armbands."

"Yeah?"

"Liz and I went to the flicks the other day, and the Pathé News showed a group of Germans wearing them. The armbands are used by a political party called the National Socialists."

They went into the Deutsche Bank. Alec stayed by the door, waiting for Frank to get served. No one else was there. The bank clerk looked first at Alec and then at Frank. He looked unsettled.

"Sprechen sie Englisch?" Frank asked. "I want to change some money." The man said nothing, so Frank made his request in German. "Ich muss etwas Geld von Englisch auf Deutsch umtauschen," He reached into his inside pocket for his wallet. The clerk looked startled and reached under the counter. He pulled out a gun and aimed it unsteadily at Frank's head.

Frank raised his hands. "Was ist los?" he asked.

"Wache, komm schnell her," shouted the clerk. A guard came from behind a recess in the wall. He, too, had a handgun raised.

"Überprüfen Sie seine Taschen," the clerk said. At which the guard stepped up to Frank and patted his pockets.

"Und die Innentaschen," said the clerk.

The guard, wearing a uniform something like that of a policeman and one of the red armbands, opened Frank's jacket and examined the inside pockets.

"Keine Waffen," the guard said to the clerk.

The clerk pointed to Alec. "Und überprüfen Sie den Mann da drüben."

With his gun raised, the guard approached Alec and patted him down.

"Er ist klar," the guard called.

The bank clerk nodded and spoke English with a heavy German accent. "I am sorry. Your friend remained by the door as if as a guard while you were to steal money." Hearing this, Alec thought it best to stay put by the door.

Frank was angry. "OK, so now you have checked us, put the damn gun away. Will you give me fifty Marks? How many English Pounds do you want?" He wasn't a walkover. Frank Bates played Rugger for Coventry and was used to rough and tumble. He felt like hitting the guard but held back, the guard and the bank clerk being armed. Apart from this, Liz implored him to be careful. He was missing her.

The money exchange was made, and the two engineers left the bank.

* * *

Frank Bates talked to his grandson some years later, recounting his travels. *"The eyes of that man bored into my head. They were positively evil. The Nazi leaders were in the Excelsior Hotel in Berlin. They planned for Hitler to stay there after he was elected as Chancellor. The Hitler swine spoke to me. If I'd had a gun—"*

"Yes, Grandpa, I understand how you must have felt, but I wouldn't be here if you'd had a gun. Anyway, what did Hitler say to you?"

"He told me where the Deutsche Bank was. So Alec Webster and I went there, and the damn bank clerk pulled a gun on us. He thought we were going to rob the place. It wasn't a good day."

Installing and testing Alfred Herbert's Capstan lathes in Siberian Omsk and Tomsk went as planned. Sensibly, the test bay team didn't stop in Berlin on the way back to England. Frank never told Liz about the gun episode in the bank.

"Want to go with Frank and Liz to the pictures tonight, love?" Alec asked Sadie after he arrived home. "The Four Horsemen of the Apocalypse is on at The Barn. Valentino's in it."

Halfway through the show, the Pathé news came on, and Adolf Hitler was seen strutting around with his cohorts. Frank leant close to Liz and told her he had met the man they saw on the screen in the Hotel Excelsior.

* * *

As the 1930s progressed, a king died. Another king began to reign, but only for a few months until he abdicated, intending to marry the woman he loved. Edward the Eighth's brother, Albert Frederick Arthur George, Bertie to those close to him, became King George the Sixth on the eleventh of December, 1936.

As the thirties progressed, there were significant fluctuations in financial markets worldwide. In some parts of Great Britain, the financial situation for families was dire. In other areas of the country, depending on the type of local industry, things were not perfect, but they were stable. An oddity of the 1930s was that although finance was not dependable, the housing market boomed. In fact, the number of houses built broke records, and those able to buy a home, although generally heavily mortgaged, had a modicum of security.

Chapter 35

1936-1939

An Allotment, a Legend, and Great Unrest

"I wouldn't mind getting an allotment," Alec told Sadie.

Next Saturday, they walked to Allesley Old Road Allotments. The site manager, Norman Cotton, showed them the vacant plots. "There's another one down this lane." He turned to the right. At the bottom of the lane, a narrow path led to a plot overgrown with weeds. Nevertheless, it had a substantial-looking garden shed and a fruit cage. Plot 432 was on a gentle slope leading to a stream.

"This is the stream that runs through Canley Ford," the manager said, with a knowing look in his eye. "You know Canley Ford?"

"It's near that new pub on the Fletchamstead Highway," Alec said.

"Isn't that place called *The Phantom Coach*?" Sadie said.

"Yes. It is. Do you know why it's called *The Phantom Coach*?"

"I've no idea," said Sadie. "Do you know?"

"I do. Look, there are some seats in the shed in this plot. It's the best vacant plot on the site. If you like, we can look at what garden tools are there. We can chat about renting a plot, and I'll tell you about the Phantom Coach."

The conversation was an odd introduction to the allotment plot that became a lifesaver to Alec and Sadie Webster. The tale told by the site manager was about a reckless coach driver, forcing his horses, foaming at the mouth, at a crazy pace down the lane that eventually became the Fletchamstead Highway. The passengers were screaming fearfully. Then suddenly, the driver lost control. The coach veered off the road and tumbled into what the locals called *A bottomless pond*, sinking without a trace.

Another version of the tale the allotment manager told Alec and Sadie was that the coach was heading down a wooded lane to Canley Ford. After entering the ford, the driver, apparently called Charlie, lost control. As a result, the coach disappeared into the nearby marshy land.

"Who knows whether it's true," Norman said. "But some people say they've heard the sound of galloping hooves."

"Hence the name of the pub," said Alec.

"Yeah. I tell you what, I want nothing to do with it. There's no telling where getting involved with that sort of stuff could lead." Although it was sunny, he shivered and went out of the shed. "Anyway, what do you think of the plot?"

They walked back up the lanes to the allotment shop. Alec signed the agreement to maintain the plot well, paid the year's rent, and then he and Sadie strolled to the Royal Oak in Earlsdon. "That old spade will come in handy again," Alec said when they sat in the lounge.

* * *

"As soon as I saw him at that hotel in Berlin, I knew Hitler couldn't be trusted," Frank Bates said to Liz. He turned the sound down on the radio. There had been an ominous news broadcast telling of German troops marching into the Sudetenland in Czechoslovakia. The Prime Minister, Neville Chamberlain, had returned to England boasting that he had acquired *'Peace in our time.'*

Frank re-tuned the radio to *Grand Hotel.* The Palm Court Orchestra made a change from the grim news. Europe, once again, was unsettled. Hitler was determined to spread the German nation's borders as far as possible.

"What do you think will happen, Frank?" Liz said.

"It looks bad. Things are going on a war footing again. I've heard that the boss of Austin, Len Lord, has asked the Prime Minister if he wants Austin to produce aircraft or tanks. It was decided that aircraft would be best."

"Is it that bad?"

"Unfortunately, it is. And there's talk of conscription."

"Oh no." Her heart skipped a beat, and suddenly she felt faint. Their four sons were old enough to be called up to join the armed forces.

* * *

"We'd better make an air-raid shelter while there's still time," Frank said to one of his sons, Harold, a self-employed builder. "We'll have it well away from the stream; we don't want the shelter to get flooded. Frank said. "It could be the emergency home to several people if air raids start, so I want it deep and large. Twelve feet wide, twenty long, and twelve feet deep should suffice."

"Be a good idea to have a toilet," Harold advised. "And running water and electricity."

"So we'd better get a generator for emergency power."

"OK, I'll get the brickwork done. You'll need to have a reinforced concrete roof, too. I would suggest at least thirty inches thick. Could you get the steel for reinforcing from the scrap at Herbert's?"

"Should be able to. I'm well-in with the Old Man."

Frank got his Test-bay team to help him construct the shelter. Within six months, working at weekends, the air-raid shelter was completed. Eighteen steps led down to a steel-faced door, across which was a ribbon. There was a grand opening one Saturday evening, during which those involved in the construction and their wives enjoyed wine, beer, sandwiches and gramophone music.

"Come on, Liz cut the ribbon," Frank called. She came down the steps and smiled when he passed her some scissors. They were alone at the door of the bomb shelter.

"You are a good man, Frank, to have done this for people's protection. I love you for the man you are."

"And I love you, Liz, from the day I first met you." They kissed each other, and those coming down the steps cheered.

"Here's the young couple," shouted Alec Webster as Liz opened the door to the shelter. The light was on and illuminating the sizeable underground room, where, in the far wall, were two open doors beyond which were a kitchen and a bathroom area.

"This is marvellous, Frank," said Liz. "But I hope we don't have to use it for the purpose it was built."

"Me too. But it's better to be safe than sorry. So come on down, you people," he called. "Come and have a look. There's food and drink here."

Chapter 36

1939-1945

Dig for Victory and Conflagration

Once again, rising tensions in Europe reached boiling point. Neville Chamberlain, the British Prime Minister, had spent months trying to persuade Hitler to rein in his obsession with expanding German territory. Finally, on the fifteenth of September 1938, The Premier flew to meet Hitler at his home, The Berghof, to moderate the German leaders' expansionist plans. The attempt failed.

The British Government had promised military protection for Poland. A crisis point was reached when the German army marched into Poland on the first of September 1939. Hitler was given an ultimatum, which he ignored. Therefore, on the third of September, 1939, the Premier, Neville Chamberlain, broadcast to the nation at eleven o'clock in the morning. He said;

'I am speaking to you from the cabinet room at Ten Downing Street. This morning the British ambassador in Berlin handed the German Government a final note stating that unless we heard from them by 11 o'clock, that they were prepared at once to withdraw their troops from Poland, a state of war would exist between us. I have to tell you now that no such undertaking has been received, and that consequently this country is at war with Germany.'

* * *

Alec Webster went to the radio and switched it off. "Well, that's it," he said to Sadie and their son, Vincent.

"Good job you're in a reserved occupation, Vince," he said. "Otherwise, you'd be in uniform and off to batter that Hitler."

In October 1939, posters produced by the Ministry of Food were placed in public places. On them were the words, *Dig for Victory*, and there were radio broadcasts which included recipes encouraging people to be self-sufficient with their provision of food. By this time, Alec, Sadie, and Vince, who took delight in digging the well-conditioned loamy soil, were established in their allotment. The first season's crops had been plentiful.

There had been a minor setback. The handle of the spade Alec had bought from auction had broken. A layer of grain in the long shank of the handle had opened.

"I'll see to it, Dad," Vince said, taking the spade home to work on it. "I'll use instrument-making wood glue," he said to Alec. "It's the strongest animal glue you can get." He heated the glue in a paint kettle over a gas ring on the cooker and quickly took it to the shed. He forced some glue into the split with a putty knife, put the handle into his vice, and as he tightened it up, the break closed, and glue oozed out of the split.

"OK, we'll leave that till tomorrow to harden off, and then I'll sand the handle down."

"Probably we ought to put a screw in to ensure the split holds together," Alec suggested.

"Better to use a tapered dowel; I'll do that now," Vince said. "This spade is a nice tool. We'll repair it in a way that keeps its character. I did think of changing the handle to a new one, but that would spoil its look. See the figuring of the grain and the patination? It only comes with the passage of time." Vince indicated the contrasting dark and light colours of the ash handle.

In Coventry, the sirens sounded at 7.00 in the evening of the fourteenth of November 1940. Frank and Liz glanced at each other and headed down the garden to the air-raid shelter. Three of Frank's sons and the three of the Test-bay team arrived with their wives.

Just before Frank slammed the steel door shut, the drone of aircraft engines could be heard getting nearer. And then, from the direction of the town, there came awful shrieking, whistling noises, followed by loud explosions.

"Those swine are destroying our lovely old town," Frank said. Liz saw that his eyes were moist.

* * *

About four miles away from Coventry, two people were cycling toward Kenilworth. The young couple was Frank Bates' daughter and her husband. They had an arrangement with a family named Winn, who lived at Albert Street in Kenilworth, a small town with no industry, so safer than Coventry. If there was an air raid at night in Coventry, Doug and Mary would cycle to the Winn's house and spend the night there.

They were freewheeling down the hill at the side of Crackley Woods, a remnant of the Forest of Arden. They were approaching a railway bridge when a loud, pounding noise started at the far side of the bridge. It was an anti-aircraft gun. Its crew were blasting shells at enemy aircraft, picked out by searchlights. It was so busy by the anti-aircraft gun that they thought it best to wait under the bridge and shelter, as Mary thought, from the rain she could hear.

There was a lull in the activity. "OK, go on by now," one of the gun crew said. So Doug and Mary pedalled on and reached Crackley Hill, where they had a clear view of Coventry. The sky above the town was a violent flaming red, and the noise of aircraft and exploding bombs, even from five miles away, was deafening.

Doug and Mary spent a sleepless night at the Winn's. They heard the 'All-clear' siren sometime after six in the morning, and then, after breakfast, they cycled back home to Coventry. On the way to their house in Beechwood Gardens, they could hear the distant sound of fire engine bells. Other than that, there seemed to be a ghostly quiet compared to the noise during the night.

As they cycled down the lane to their house they saw their next-door neighbour, Bert Green. He was in his Auxiliary Fire Brigade uniform and looked tired, dishevelled and smudged with soot. He waved them down.

"It's been a bad night, over two hundred fires," he said, "There was a firestorm. The city centre's gone, including the Cathedral. There are fires still burning. The Jerries had a go at some of the factories."

"Which ones?" Doug asked. He was a reserved occupation electrician, one of the many local tradesmen responsible for keeping Shadow Factories running.

"I've heard that Triumph, Daimler, Humber and Alfred Herbert have been destroyed. Some of the aircraft factories have been severely damaged. The damage is widespread."

"So it's a good job we've got the Shadow Factories running on the outskirts then," Doug responded.

"It is. Are you working today, Doug?"

"Later on. Reynold Chain today. Before that, Mary and I'll go and see what damage they've done."

"I wouldn't go in the town if I were you; I'd leave it for a few days." Bert turned to go in. Tears were on his cheeks.

"You OK?" Doug called after him.

"No. Terrible things happened last night. Four hundred and forty-nine bombers were counted. They came in several waves. The dead are in the streets. People are alive under the rubble. You can hear them. Don't go into the town, Doug.

Doug was quick on the uptake. "Let's go for a pint tonight."

"Good idea. I'm not on duty tonight, and I need a pint and a few whiskeys to drown the bloody memories. Where shall we go?"

"The Phantom Coach."

After their shift, Doug working at the Chain and Bert at the Standard, they and their wives walked half a mile down Canley Road to the Phantom Coach. It was a peaceful night following the Blitzkrieg raid, from which the term 'Coventrated' was coined. The area around the Phantom Coach was undamaged, which at least helped the morale of the four in a minor way. Even though the general conversation in the pub was angry about the *Damn Germans* and other more Anglo-Saxon descriptions. A drink was ordered, and then another. They were very much enjoyed, and during the half-mile walk back home, Doug thought the surroundings looked somewhat fuzzy.

Chaos reigned in Great Britain for the next four and a half years. People grew more able, mentally, to deal with the danger. But, it was never far away, and sometimes the bestiality of war was thrown at people when the ones they loved died.

Frank Bates eldest son, Reg, died. He had volunteered to join the Air Force and became a rear gunner in a Vickers Wellington Bomber. It was shot down in a raid over Berlin, and Frank never got over it. Later on in life, long after he retired from Alfred Herbert's, he was asleep in an armchair when his youngest grandson visited him. The young man touched his grandfather's arm, which woke Frank up with a start. "Oh, Reg," the old man cried joyfully, thinking his son had returned. So many memories were made, and so many people were lost.

* * *

One evening after the German surrender in 1945, Doug and Mary took their two-year-old son into Broadgate, Coventry City centre. It was packed with people, and lights, non-existent for six years, were shining brightly everywhere, illuminating the surviving buildings. Music was playing, and people were laughing and joking. The bells of Holy Trinity church, which had been silent for the duration of the war, were ringing their clarion of base and treble loud and clear. A soldier in uniform turned and saw Doug's son on his Dad's shoulders. "It's over, sonny-Jim," said the soldier, with a broad smile that stuck in the boy's memory for the rest of his life.

Chapter 37

1945-1959

Raising the Past

In a 1914 Times editorial, the author, H.G. Wells, had said that the conflict that had commenced would be *The war that will end war*. When the Second World War killing stopped with the German surrender on the eighth of May, 1945, a sort of perverse poetry took place. The Axis military chiefs signed the instrument of surrender in the same railway carriage used after the First World War.

Coventry's industrial might began to blossom quickly after World War Two. Workers from all over Great Britain and abroad heard about industrial Coventry and headed there. Not that this situation was new. Throughout the ages, the City of Coventry had the propensity to forge ahead with new industries. The city's guilds represented different industries, and apprentices would become what was called a Journeyman after their time as an apprentice was served. They would also become a Freeman of the City, allowing them to graze their horses on local common land free of charge. In addition, they would be entitled to 'The City Hundred', one hundred pounds to help them start their own business. The aim of this was to generate productivity. The method worked through hundreds of years into the nineteen fifties, where we again pick up the story about Thomas Satchwell's spade.

The year was 1952. Princess Elizabeth Mountbatten-Windsor, and her husband, Prince Philip, Duke of

Edinburgh, were on tour. They were first going to Kenya, from where they would go to Australia and then to New Zealand.

After a night at Treetops Hotel in Kenya, the couple returned to where they were staying, Sagana Lodge. They were informed that the Princess's father, King George the Sixth, had died. He had been ill for a while, and the Princess had represented him officially many times; now she was Queen, and a new age began.

In their later years, Alec and Sadie Webster's plot at Allesley Old Road Allotments became a haven for them. Their plot, number 432, was way into the site, near a wild area where foxes, badgers, and many different species of birds roamed freely.

Alec and Sadie joined the 'Allotment Gang' who met every Wednesday evening at the Royal Oak on the corner of Moor Street in Earlsdon. Their son, Vince Webster, had spare time on his hands, and his interests widened out. He wanted a complete change, and being interested in the history of Coventry for a long while, he joined The Coventry Local History Society.

The Society met fortnightly at a public house called The Nursery Tavern, on Lord Street, in the Coventry district of Chapelfields. The group met on Wednesday evenings in the lounge bar, and Vince decided to go early as it was his first meeting. One other person, a girl, was sitting on the other side of the room. Vince went to her, introduced himself, and she responded with the brightest smile and told him her name was Jennie Whitehouse.

They sat together throughout the meeting, during which a local archaeologist discussed in detail a village long since gone near the Charterhouse on the London Road.

"There is still preparation work we must do," said Howard Cafelle. "But in conclusion, I will say that the excavation of the village thought to have had the name, Shortley, will be one of the most interesting digs there has been around here."

"Would you like to get involved with that?" Vince whispered to Jennie. She nodded.

"That dig was the main reason I came to this meeting. It's the first time I've come here," Jennie whispered, leaning close to him. He thought how pleasant she was. "I saw the title of the talk on a poster in the library. I'll tell you more when the meeting's finished."

Ten minutes later, the session drew to a close, with the chairman announcing the theme of the next meeting. Jennie and Vince went further down the room, away from other people. He ordered drinks, and they settled down for a chat. She told him what interested her in coming to the Historical Society's meeting.

"It's only family hearsay, but my Grandad told me that some of our ancestors came from a village called Shortley."

"Did he give you any more details?"

"Apparently, they lived in a manor there."

"Did they own it?"

"I've no idea."

"The more information you can find out by word of mouth, the better it would be."

"I would ask him if I could. But he died two years ago."

"Oh, Jen, I'm sorry to hear that." He paused, not wanting to appear forward. "Maybe I can help. We could get involved with the dig when it starts."

"That would be lovely," Jennie looked at her watch. "I'm

sorry, Vince; I've got to go and catch the bus now."

"OK, I'll walk to the bus stop with you."

At the bus stop, they chatted and told each other about their interests. Jennie told Vince about studying architectural and general history in her spare time. "It was after I heard our family might be connected to that manor in Shortley that I became interested in history."

"Coventry's local history is fascinating. So much has happened here over the years."

As well as history, Vince and Jennie loved the outdoors. They began to meet at a local dance hall and soon became inseparable. The theme of one of the Historical Society's meetings was Anglo-Saxon Coventry. "Throughout the ages," the speaker said, "The River Sherbourne was central to the life of the city, its tradespeople, and its citizens. But unfortunately, the river also figured in the 1849 cholera epidemic that swept through the town because the Sherbourne was the dumping ground for effluent and waste products from the city's population and industry. Ironically, in Anglo-Saxon times, the name of the Sherbourne was Scire Burnan or Clear River." The speaker pointed to the board where he had written 'Sherbourne'.

"You can see here how the sound of the name, Scire Burnan evolved into the modern 'Sherbourne'."

"As most locals know, the river still meanders through the city. But with the town's growth, it has mainly been built over and is observable in only a few places. As a result, its route through the town is an absorbing mystery to those of us interested in local history."

What the speaker mentioned immediately gave Vince a challenge. He had an adventurous spirit, but he kept quiet about the idea until the session finished, and they moved to where the room was more peaceful.

"I've got a suggestion," he said to Jennie. He was smiling mischievously.

"Tell me then."

"It's about the Sherbourne."

"Really?"

"Fancy a walk?"

"What do you mean, along the river? There's no path."

"The walk will be in the river, the underground parts."

"But no one has been there for years, as far as I know."

"That's the point. There's no telling what we'll find."

"Vince, the depth would be higher than my Wellingtons."

"I've got some waders, and we can get some for you from Lynes' Stores."

One Sunday evening, after dark, when all was quiet, Vince parked the car in Well Street, near Lynes Stores, a short walk from Palmer Lane, where there was a short exposed part of the Sherbourne. The way into the river was down a steep bank consisting of the stone foundations of a long-demolished building. They cautiously made their way through the brick arch of Palmer Lane, creeping along the cobbles to a gap in the railings on the river's edge. They slipped on the waders. Vince hoisted a small rucksack onto his shoulders, and they climbed down the stonework of the bank and eased themselves into the water.

Jennie breathed a sigh of relief when she felt the cold water only reach above her knees. She grasped Vincent's hand as they slowly entered the tunnel where the river went under the archway below Palmer Lane.

Vince looked to where they climbed down the bank. No one was coming down the lane, so he switched on his torch and handed another to Jennie. "I've got spare batteries and bulbs, so we won't run out of light." He shone his torch ahead. The light picked out ancient brickwork, some of it covered in algae. They waded along the river, checking their footing as they went, eventually coming to a left-hand bend where the wall was made of irregular stone blocks, which were a dark red colour.

"That's Warwickshire Sandstone, foundations of a building if I'm not mistaken," Jennie said, focussing her torch on an area of red stonework. The river, coursing against the stonework for hundreds of years, had worn the stone smooth to about two feet above the river's present level. Higher up, the stone mason's tool marks were still visible.

A few yards further on, a pile of sandstone was picked out on the right in the dim torch light. The stone blocks had fallen from the wall into the river. As they approached the rubble, they could see a large hole that looked black and cavernous partway up the wall.

"This is eerie," Jennie said, looking at the curved roof, a mixture of brick and stone. "I wonder what's happened there."

"I've no idea." They reached the fallen stones and gazed up into what appeared to be another tunnel in the wall some six feet above them. They shone their torches into the blackness.

"Are you up for this, Jen?"

"I certainly am. Lead on."

They scrambled up the pile of stones, Vince helping Jennie over the ones at the top. The tunnel at the top of the fallen stonework was spacious, its floor, picked out in the torchlight, leading off at a slight incline at right angles to the course of the river.

"Shall we follow this now or come back another time?" Jen asked as she stepped further into the tunnel. She shone her torch ahead and saw some architectural features, a window, and a doorway, the top of which was styled in Gothic fashion. Jennie thought the tunnel was odd, out of place, historically, as she looked ahead in the dim torchlight.

"I think we should investigate it now."

"So do I. It's a major find. Just look at it." She shone her torch ahead. "At one time, this was a lane on the surface. There are even cobbles here." Jen walked a few paces. Vince followed, shining his torch on the ground. He saw the cobbles were worn.

"With how these stones are worn, this street was a major thoroughfare at one time. He shone his torch higher. "It's like the place is frozen in time." They walked on, passed a wooden door set deep into the stonework and came to some stone-mullioned windows.

"It reminds me of a book I read," said Jennie, in an undertone. "It was 'The House Under the Water'. A village in a Welsh valley was lost when the valley became a reservoir."

"And here we have a lost street."

Jen nodded and stopped to look around. "The book was written by Francis Brett Young. He was from Halesowen."

"Where's Halesowen?"

"In the Black Country. Before heavy industry took over, the Black Country was green and beautiful."

Vince liked how Jen expressed herself. He shone his torch through a window to illuminate the blackness inside. There was a table with four chairs around it and two other chairs near a large fireplace. On the two chairs were the remnants of cushions covered in mould. On the table, four plates were in front of the chairs where people had been sitting; cutlery was scattered untidily, as were the chairs.

"Look at this, Jen."

Jennie had been trying to recall what she had learned about building styles of the past. The street was medieval, but precisely what period . . . she thought the buildings looked very similar to the ones in Bayley lane, which were from fourteen to the fifteenth century. She took her gaze away from the dark void of the street ahead and went to see what Vince had found.

"I think they made a hurried exit," he said. "Look up the street, there on the left." He focused his torch on the entrance to a half-timbered house where a door hung open, motionless. Other entries were also ajar when Vince and Jennie walked along the street. Household effects lay scattered around. Children's wooden toys lay on the ground at the threshold of one of the buildings.

"Look," Jen pointed up ahead. A sword lay on the ground. The steel was rusty, but the brass parts of the handle were in reasonable condition. Lying by the sword were some items of clothing, a sash, and a cape; just within the open doorway was a helmet made of steel. Vince gently picked up the sword and helmet and Jennie the clothing.

"I think this equipment will help us date when the street was covered over. It's part of a soldier's uniform. The colours of the sash will determine the regiment and the date this uniform was being used—"

"—If we're able to see the correct colours."

"Yeah, but don't forget there's been no sunlight here, so the fading should be minimised."

"True."

"That helmet, by the way, is a Cabasset."

"Where did you learn all this stuff, Jen?"

"Night school for the architecture, self-taught in the reference library and Encyclopaedia Britannica for the rest." She smiled at him. "It's been fascinating, but this place takes first prize. And it's good fun."

"But rather creepy fun."

"Unfortunately, yes." Jen glanced at Vince and then looked ahead into the dim distance of the street, poorly lit by her torch. The lane was strewn with artefacts from a bygone age, and she shivered. "It's as if we're in a time capsule, and it's so silent, apart from the sound of the river back there."

"I know what you mean. It's as if there ought to be people here, still populating the place. Going about their daily business."

"I think I know what happened."

"Really?"

"Back in 1575, there was an outbreak of bubonic plague in several places in England, York, Norwich, Bristol; places that were busy, industrially, where people went with their wares, and where they obtained raw materials for their products. And where else was busy industrially at the time?"

"Coventry?"

"Exactly. And a sudden onset of the plague would explain what looks like a hasty departure of folks from this street."

"And if the plague was particularly virulent around here, it would explain why the people back then thought it best to cover the street, effectively to bury it."

"There's another thing I've noticed."

Vincent stopped and regarded the person he had grown so close to. He went to her and drew her to him, holding her tight. In this dark, uneasy place, he felt he had to reassure her and make her feel safe. "I've noticed how thankful I am to have met you, Jennie Whitehouse, but what will we do now?"

"What do you mean?"

"What will we do about our find? Are we even supposed to be here? This find is so important. It could be a tourist attraction for the town. Jen, I've been considering standing as a Councillor for Coventry as an Independent. One of my thoughts is that the Sherbourne, the Scire Burnan, should be seen again throughout the town. This place could be added to the attraction."

"That would be lovely, Vince. These shops and houses could be restored and used again. Imagine that. There could be a restaurant here and a pub called the Scire Burnan. Let's work on it together."

"And there's something else we ought to work on together. We should get engaged. Will you marry me, Jennie Whitehouse?"

Chapter 38

1959-1965

Boom Time, Cuba and a Nature Reserve.

A by-election took place, and Vince Webster became an Independent Councillor. He tried to get his proposal passed to landscape Coventry by exposing the Sherbourne and planting trees along its course. However, with the volume of cars coming off the assembly lines in Coventry and Birmingham and the public's desire to own a car, parking was becoming a problem in the city centre. New car parks were more critical than the landscaping that most councillors called 'town decoration'. As a result, Vince and Jennie agreed to keep the underground discovery to themselves. "If they don't want to beautify the town, I'm not going to reveal our find," Vince told Jennie after his proposal was kicked out.

Councillor Webster no longer had the time to maintain his parents' allotment, and they didn't have the energy to work on it. So the place that gave contentment and abundant crops, allotment 432, was vacated. Within a few months, it became overgrown with weeds.

Two seasons went by, and then one Saturday in late January of 1959, a problem arose that needed dealing with urgently. The allotment site manager, Ted Briggs, suggested to the other three committee members that they have a beer at The Oak to discuss things. Nationally, there was talk of Councils taking back allotment land that, for hundreds of years, had been the commoners' right to hold for a modest payment. In Coventry, many vacant plots were at the Allesley Old Road allotment site. Ted had been

216

worried that the Council might hijack the site, so he wrote to them to clarify the matter.

* * *

"It's my round," Ted said to the others. He ordered the usual beers, and when they were settled at their table, he explained the problem.

"There is a need for housing, and allotment sites over the country are being grabbed by Councils. I've been hoping the Council wouldn't shut us down and grab all of our site."

"Do you think they'll try and take it off us?" asked Mike Partiss.

Ted didn't answer the question but responded, "I had a letter from the Council a couple of weeks back. They were asking about what need there is for allotments locally. It was one of those ambiguous letters that you sometimes get from officials. I couldn't tell what they were after, but they were pumping me for information. It's been worrying, but I didn't want to say anything to you chaps at the time. It was me, being the chairman, who had to respond to the Council. They had to explain what they wanted in simple terms for me to tell you and all the plot-holders, so I waited for their response."

"You should have told us, Ted, shared the load."

"Maybe so. Anyway, a friend of mine is a solicitor. I approached him about the situation, and he helped me compose a letter."

"I think people got fed up with all the effort growing food for survival in the war years. That's why there are so many vacant plots," said Mike Partiss. "What do you think, Ralph?" Mike asked.

"I think it's due to the rise in wages in the engineering and car factories around here. People can afford to buy their vegetables these days. Besides, vegetables are being imported when they're out of season. There's no need to grow them if you don't want to."

Billy, 'Spud' Murphy, the treasurer, chimed in. "As far as money's concerned, we're not getting rent for the vacant plots. Out of the four hundred and thirty-seven plots on our site, we've got a hundred and twenty-seven that aren't used. There's no chance we four can keep them all tidy; that's a pointless exercise."

Ted Briggs nodded. "I had a reply from the Parks Department this morning." He took an envelope out of his pocket, had a draught of beer, and summarised the letter. "They're suggesting we only hand back the vacant land to the Council. They also suggest, and I think this is a brilliant idea, that the land we give back would be turned into a nature reserve. There's a need for one in the City. There's also enough vacant land around Coventry for new housing, so they aren't trying to grab the whole site off us."

There were murmurs of approval.

"That would be a good outcome," Spud said. "It would take the onus off us to maintain the plots that aren't being used."

"And it would be good for the community to have a nature reserve within the town, as long as everyone can access it. But there is a problem." Ralph could see a complication.

"What's the problem?" Ted asked.

"The vacant plots are all over the site. So for this nature reserve idea to work, the land we return to the Council would have to be in one area at the edge of the site. Now, some allotment holders wouldn't mind giving up their plot and moving to a different part of the site, but others, maybe some of those who have had their plot for years, wouldn't like that."

"But the land does belong to the Council. Somehow, I don't know how, they've got wind of the spare land in our site, and they want it utilised. Officialdom can be dogmatic sometimes, and I think, if plot-holders said they weren't prepared to shift to a different plot, the Council could dig their heels in and maybe take the whole lot off us."

"So let's put it to a vote," the chairman said. "Those in favour of giving the Council the same amount of plots on the edge of the site as the plots that are vacant, raise your hand." All four agreed, with the proviso, that everyone in the community should be allowed access to the nature reserve.

A circular outlining the changes was sent to all of the allotment holders. The majority agreed to the proposal, including those who needed to move to a different plot. However, that decision was made more attractive with the resolution that the ones having to move would have the first year rent-free in their new plot.

By the time autumn came, with the onset of early frosts, the changes were complete. A new boundary fence was installed at the Council's cost. Most of the gates and fences were removed from the perimeter of the vacated allotments. Sheds were sold or left on site, and some dismantled, to be burned in a nearby field on the next Guy Fawkes Night.

The disused plots, without cultivation, soon returned to the wild. As the seasons went by, they became the haunt of foxes, badgers, and birds of prey. The nature reserve, Grays Wood, with its old allotment lanes, became a favourite for locals who loved a walk.

Some of them would take along a knapsack or a carrier bag, for there was a bonus on this walk along the old pathways. Fruit trees still grew in abundance in those forgotten places. Apples, pears and plums were there for the taking. In the occasional corner, one would catch sight of floral displays in disused flower beds that, in due season, teased the eyes with riotous colour.

* * *

On Friday, October 26th, 1962, a nineteen-year-old apprentice named Ross Watts was washing his new Austin Mini outside the factory where he worked in Leamington Spa. The news over the past few days had been dire. An American U2 spy plane, flying at a great height over the island of Cuba, ninety miles from mainland America, had photographed the installation of Russian nuclear missiles.

The World, and Ross Watts, were on edge. He glanced in the direction of Coventry. The sky was a clear blue, hardly fitting for the oppressive tension everyone felt. It would be more fitting if its colour was the black of night.

If war happened, Coventry, like it had been twenty-two years before, would be a target because of its resurgence onto the world stage as a place of industrial might. Ross thought of his girl in Coventry. He had met her at a dance school not long ago and wanted to always be with her. Laura Hall never left his thoughts. How could any nation's leader be so cruel as to threaten their life together?

Behind the scenes at this point, unknown to most of the World's population, Nikita Khrushchev, the Russian leader, had written to the American President, John Fitzgerald Kennedy, outlining a plan to enable the two superpowers to step back from the brink.

By November 20th, after the most fraught time in human history, when the doomsday clock had reached a few seconds before midnight, the two major powers eased off the warmongering. Peace of a sort descended upon the Earth. Ross Watts could see his girl at the Gaumont that evening and watch the film 'A Summer Place' without the fear of annihilation. There had been a great lesson learned from the Cuban crisis. Ross and Laura resolved to ensure they enjoyed the simple pleasures of life, those innocent pleasures everyone should enjoy while they had time with those they love.

They enjoyed the film immensely and decided to go for a walk when they met the following Saturday. "With the threat of the past few days gone, a walk would be lovely," said Ross.

"Yes, I know. To wind down."

"It'll be cold. The weather report says frost's coming."

"Doesn't matter. I've got a nice warm coat that I haven't worn yet. It's an autumn green waterproof with a hood. Green's one of my colours, along with russet."

"I like autumn colours too. So where shall we go for a walk? Anywhere you fancy?"

"I know a place that isn't far away."

"Where is it?"

"Going toward the Allesley side of town. It's a nature reserve. Dad told me it's large, a bit quaint in places, but *very* interesting," Laura said.

* * *

The precision-tool-making factory owned by his uncle, where Ross worked in Leamington Spa, was an ancient building. It was built in the late seventeen hundreds when Leamington's Spa water was gaining a reputation as a healer of ills. The factory had been home to different businesses. A blacksmith had his forge there. Rumour was that the elephants on tour were housed in the building many years ago when the circus was in Leamington. It was also where Frank Whittle, the jet engine inventor, had a workshop.

Ross could tell the place was old. The stairs creaked when he walked up them. The brickwork was far from modern, and the interior style of the building was that of yesteryear. The ceiling of the ground floor workshop rooms were the oak floorboards, grey with age, of the upstairs rooms.

During lunchtime, two days before Ross and Laura met for the walk in the Grays Wood nature reserve, Ross was sitting by a radiator backing onto a brick pillar in the ground-floor machine shop. The weather forecast for the day had been correct. It was still frosty even though it was past noon, and the hot radiator was welcome. Two other people were huddling by it, Ross's father, Arthur, who supervised the factory, and Barry Connolly, a seventeen-year-old. No one else was in the building. The large front door was closed, effectively locked. Without a Yale key, no one could enter.

Whenever Arthur went up the main stairway to his office, which could also be accessed by a narrow stairway at the rear of the building, his footsteps would be heard on the floor above. His chair would be heard scraping the floorboards as he dragged it away from his desk to sit down. Which made what happened next threatening and very odd. Measured footsteps could be heard on the floor above, and the office chair was dragged out.

The point is that Arthur was downstairs, not in his office. Arthur was a Special Police Sergeant then and would take no messing. He frowned at Ross, who glanced at Barry, and as the three stood. Arthur quietly stated his orders as he grabbed a nearby steel bar to use as a truncheon. "I'll stay by the door to stop them getting out. Ross, you take the back stairs. Barry, you go up the front stairs." Ross and Barry headed upstairs, prepared for a rough and tumble.

They rushed to Arthur's office. No one was there. The chair they heard being dragged out from the desk was still where it should be, tucked under the desk. So they searched the upper floor meticulously. No interloper was found.

"I don't get this. We heard someone up there," Barry said as they returned to Arthur, waiting, cudgel in hand, by the front door. "Nobody's up there," Ross said. "I can't weigh this up, dad; the three of us heard footsteps."

"And the chair moved; the three of us heard it," Arthur ruminated, chin in hand. And then, "Let's sit down; I've got something to tell you."

Ross and Barry were curious about what was to follow as the three of them settled close to the radiator.

"What's happened ties in with other strange goings-on."

"You haven't told Mum and me about anything strange that's gone on." Ross felt a touch colder and pulled his chair closer to the radiator.

"No, I haven't, but I can't avoid telling you, now we've all experienced something unusual. Things go on here that occasionally stretch the imagination. I was working here alone not long after Vernon bought the place. I'd finished wiring the machines up and was ready to knock off. As true as I'm sitting here, I smelt pipe tobacco. It took me back to when I was a kid. My father had a friend who came occasionally. He was a pipe smoker. He smoked old-fashioned stuff they called shag tobacco. Anyway, no one was here apart from me, but the strong smell of pipe tobacco wafted over to me.

"There was another occasion. At the time, two of us were working here, Harold Watson and me. Harold, about seventy at the time, was working the shaping machine, that one, over there. I was working at the bench," Arthur pointed to a vice where he sometimes still worked. "So, you see, me and Harold Watson were about five yards apart. I was filing the rads on some eighteen-inch height gauge bases and suddenly felt a punch in the back. It was like a punch with a vengeance. I turned around, and old Harold was still working the shaper with his back to me. At first, I thought Harold had done it, but obviously, he hadn't because he was so far away."

"Did you tell Harold about it?" Barry asked.

"I did. And I asked if he'd heard or seen anything, but he hadn't."

"What do you think it is?"

"I don't know. But here's some advice for you two. Keep well away from that stuff. Ghosts and witch-craft are the thin ends of the wedge that lead to nasty demonic stuff that could get out of control."

"Do you believe that?" asked Barry.

"I do, and I'll tell you why. An ancient book that's got plenty of good advice warns us to keep away from that stuff. It could get out of hand. But that's for another time. We need to get back to work, Barry and Ross. So if anything weird happens around here, keep out of it, and let me know."

"What will you do, dad, make an arrest?"

Arthur grinned. "Yeah, I might well do that."

* * *

Ross picked Laura up in the Mini on Saturday morning. After he parked the car, it was a short walk over some grassland to Grays Wood nature reserve's perimeter, where a path led into its interior. Although still cold, it was a sunny day, where luxuriant, dappled areas of light and shade created beauty in the overgrown allotment plots on each side of the old pathways.

The remnants of hedges and gates were evident. It took little imagination to visualise the allotment owners still at work tending their plots. Ross stopped by a broken gate, where there was a path to an orchard. A stream was trickling its timeless way at the side of the old allotment plot, which was now a wilderness.

"This reminds me of some poetry I wrote a little while ago," Ross said. Laura saw the look on his face. He was entranced by the wild beauty.

"I didn't know you wrote, least of all, poetry," Laura said. Sometimes Ross surprised Laura with his accomplishments, much like she surprised him.

"It's the first poem I've written for a while, he said. I'm attempting to write a novel now, a historical one."

"Do you remember the poem?" Laura came to Ross's side and leaned her head on his shoulder.

"I'll try . . ." He remembered the poem, and as he recited it, Laura felt she was transported into a different realm.

* * *

'And Yggdrasil slumbered
In the glades of the forest
In Old-times numbered
One to seven.

And then she awoke
With the eyes of an eagle,
And a countenance to evoke
A trace of Heaven.

Yggdrasil speeds in the dimming light,
Fast she runs through the gathered gloaming
Sending all harm to flight
' Til her paths are bright and golden.

And Yggdrasil, the woodland sprite
Is Victress over the dark of night.'"

"Oh, Ross, that's beautiful." Laura looked into the old allotment plot they were standing by. In her imagination, she conjured a vision of Yggdrasil speeding through the old allotments. And then something caught her eye. She stepped over the broken gate with the number 432 on it and held her hand for Ross to grasp.

"Come on, Mister Keats," she said. They walked into the allotment. Weeds grew through gaps between some slabs that had been the base of a shed. A spade was lying on the ground, sheltered under what had once been a hedge. Laura picked it up. The metalwork was rusty, and the wooden handle was dull.

"Shall we take it?" Laura asked.

"Definitely. It'll be a reminder of a lovely walk."

Chapter 39

1965-1975

Apollo 11 and Elmdon Airport

Ross used emery paper to de-rust the metalwork of the spade. The process revealed two letters, *T* and *S*, stamped into the steel. He filled the letters with black paint to make them stand out, and after sanding the wooden handle, he applied Danish Oil to it, which brought out the grain.

He was pleased with the restoration. Apart from where rust had eaten into the steel and wear that gave it character, the spade looked good.

"You've made a good job of that, son." His father's words struck deep.

"You like it then, dad?"

"I do; it's a good tool." Arthur took it and felt its weight. "That'll serve you well when you've got your own place. Speaking of that, how's your young lady?"

* * *

It was 16 July 1969, and the time was one thirty-two, early morning GMT. Sitting in their living room, watching the special broadcast on television, were Ross and Laura Watts and their four-year-old son, Jamie. The six-week-old Ricky was fast asleep.

"Five . . . four . . . three . . . two . . . one . . . Zero, we have lift-off!" Millions of people worldwide focused on television screens as the mighty Saturn Five rocket lifted off with three crew-men aboard bound for the Moon.

"That rocket has got seven and a half million pounds of static thrust," Ross said as the vehicle making history arose into the blue yonder.

"Awe-inspiring," Laura quietly said as the noise of the five Rocketdyne F1 engines filled the room with noise and optimism as it lifted from Cape Canaveral.

"Where are the men?" asked Jamie.

"Up near the top." Ross went to the screen, where there was a wide-angle shot of the vehicle riding the fire. He pointed out the crew module and then sat back down. "What potential there is, Laura. This is just the start. Where will humankind be a hundred years from now?"

"Makes you wonder. It would be good to know what's up ahead. It would be good to avoid the bad and only experience the good. If only we could do that."

"Could make sense, and it would be beautiful too." Ross tried to contemplate what things would be like way into the future, what advances there would be. What undreamed of changes there would be. He looked at his wife and children. The ones he loved so much. If only they had an eternal life ahead of them in perfect health with a universe to explore. He looked at the Apollo 11 Moon Rocket again, now just a speck in the sky approaching the escape velocity of twenty-five thousand miles per hour.

Ross reached for Laura's hand and was thankful for meeting her, the beautiful woman at his side. At this pivotal point in humanity's history of exploration, he looked forward to their long life together.

Eight days of fascination followed. At a very long distance, people got to know the Commander of the Lunar Module, Neil Armstrong and the Lunar Module's Pilot, Buzz Aldrin. The pilot of the Command Module, Michael

Collins, took more of a back seat publically because he stayed in orbit for the duration of the expedition to the surface of the Moon.

The main action, including the famous phrase *'That's one small step for man, one giant leap for mankind,'* and low-gravity leaping and running by men in spacesuits, was what folks wanted to hear and see. Neil Armstrong and Buzz Aldrin gave them those things in full measure.

All too soon, the astronauts left the Moon and were on their way back to Earth.

"Will they get back alright, Dad?" asked Jamie. He had a worried look because instead of Batman and Robin being the people he would like to meet, he wanted to meet Buzz and Neil, so he hoped they would return to Earth safely.

* * *

The Apollo Lunar expeditions created an interest in space travel and flight in Jamie Watts's mind. At Jamie's young age, when the men landed on the moon, his interest was far from practical. However, as the lad became older, his interest in flight increased. When he was fifteen, Jamie joined the 84 Squadron Air Training Corps, which had a weekly meeting in Cow Lane, near the centre of Coventry.

Jamie learned all manner of things to do with aircraft and the Royal Air Force, including rifle drill, marching drill and Morse code. Going to the squadron meeting on the bus made him feel big. He was in uniform, Air Force blue trousers, a tunic with silver buttons, and a beret sporting the 84 Squadron ATC badge. And there was flying. A summer holiday week was spent at RAF Chivenor, a Hawker Hunter Squadron in North Devon. On another occasion, the squadron went to Elmdon Airport, near Birmingham, for a flight in an Avro Anson.

At Elmdon, when the flight was over, Jamie, and his friend, Alan Law, had time to kill before the Coventry bus arrived, so they went for a stroll around the airport. Two war-time Nissen Huts looked inviting because light aircraft were parked nearby. Activity suggested that a de Havilland Tiger Moth was being readied for take-off.

The two cadets stood by a chain-link fence near the Nissen Huts with an entrance sporting the sign *Maxstoke Flying Club*. A man stood at the front of the biplane. "Sucking in," he shouted, slowly rotating the propeller eight times. "Contact," he called, and then he vigorously swung the propeller, and the Gypsy Major engine kicked into life. The aircraft taxied onto a grassy area some distance from the clubhouse, turned into the wind, the engine revved up, and the Tiger Moth was airborne in a short distance.

A voice behind them startled the cadets. "What squadron are you in, lads?" the man asked. They gave him their details and explained about their flight in the Anson.

"How long were you up?"

"About ten minutes," Alan told him.

"Is that all? Maybe I can do better than that. I've got a suggestion. Come into the clubhouse; I'll explain." He opened a gate in the fence, let them in and indicated for them to follow him into an office. "Sit down, lads, get comfortable." He pointed to some chairs, and the cadets sat, wondering what the man, who had an RAF-style moustache, was about to say. He introduced himself as Julian King, the secretary of the flying club, and he asked their names.

"Well, Jamie, Alan, I've got a proposition. There are some jobs we need doing here that we haven't got time for, and I wonder if you two lads would do them for us?"

"What are the jobs?" asked the astute sixteen-year-old Alan Law, a Corporal in 84 Squadron. He wondered what the catch was and looked suspiciously at the club secretary. Alan took after his father, who never did a job for nothing.

King smiled at them, "There will be a reward if you want to help us out. What we would like you to do, maybe on Saturdays, would be to vacuum the clubhouse and keep the garden tidy. Then, after that, maybe you could give the inside of the club a lick of paint."

"You said there would be a reward," Alan said.

"Yes," King carried on. "We'll give you the occasional flight and a flying scholarship if all goes well."

There was a stunned silence in the room. And then, "What aircraft will we fly in?" asked Jamie.

"We've got two Tiger Moths, two Austers and a Provost. The Tiger Moth will be a good experience for you. An open cockpit is exhilarating when you do aerobatics."

The arrangements went well. Over the following weeks, the clubhouse was vacuumed at weekends. A start was made on the painting. Finally, the time came for the first flight in a Tiger Moth. Jamie donned a flying jacket, helmet and goggles and walked over the tarmac with the pilot.

Jamie was a reader. Some of his favourite books when he was younger, which fed his mind with thoughts of flying, were those written by Captain W.E. Johns about Biggles. He looked behind him and saw people at the window of the Observation Lounge looking at him in his flying gear.

He climbed into the passenger seat and plugged in the earphones. Then, one of the club members went through the procedure of turning the prop by hand and sucking fuel into the engine.

"Contact. Magnetos on," said the pilot. The man at the front swung the prop . . . nothing the first time. Rotated it firmly a second time, and the engine fired up. The pilot went through pre-flight checks and then taxied to the runway.

"Are you ready?" Jamie heard through the earphones. He gave the thumbs-up. "Then away we go," said the pilot, and the engine revved up. The aircraft only went a few yards along the runway until the tail lifted. They were airborne, and he felt he *was* Biggles.

On that flight, they did some minor aerobatics, dives and tight turns, and at the end of the adventurous half-hour, they landed and taxied to the front of the clubhouse.

There were several flights over the summer months. Then, one Saturday, when the clubhouse was empty of everyone but the two cadets, they went into the bar area with their paintbrushes and a tin of gloss white paint to make a start on the windows.

It was a well-stocked bar, with beer pumps, bottles of red and white wine, and bottles of spirits with optics hung on the wall at the back of the bar.

"When I was eleven," Jamie told Alan, "My grandad came to our house with Aunt Marie and had a meal. It was a special occasion, I forget what now, but there was wine, liqueur, port and sherry on the sideboard. Anyway, I think Aunt Marie had had a few Sherries, and she'd loosened up, so she gave us a song. I can still hear it now, even though it was—" Jamie worked it out— "six years ago."

"What was it, something by Vera Lynn?"

"You must be joking. It was some operatic thing, Delilah, if I remember right. *Ah, once again,* it started. My grandad was shaking his head and full of emotion during the performance, he loved it, but you've never heard such a row. I think she had a contrasto voice."

"Contralto."

"What?"

"The voice . . . contralto. A deep range in women's vocals. And the opera might have been Samson and Delilah, by Charles-Camille Saint-Saëns."

"OK, anyway, Mum and Dad took the old folks home, which left me alone with the booze."

"What happened?"

"I tried it."

"All of it?"

"Tried most of it."

"Did your Mum and Dad find out?"

"They did. I was on the floor when they got back. What do you think of this lot here?" Jamie pointed behind the bar.

"Doesn't look bad. There's a good choice."

"Fancy trying it?"

"As long as we don't end up on the floor."

"What do you want?"

"A whisky, I'll have a double."

"I will too. Bells or Jamesons?"

"Make mine a Bells, if you will, my man." Jamie poured.

Painting the clubhouse was a happy time. After double whiskies and another single each, they cleared the evidence, washing the glasses and putting them on the shelf exactly where they were before use.

"It's good they trust us to get on with the painting when they're n-not here," said Alan. He felt woozy.

Jamie looked out the window and saw the Provost taxiing to its place in front of the clubhouse. "Look sharp; they're back." He picked up his paintbrush and carried on painting the windowsill.

"Painting's looking good, lads," said the secretary when he and his passenger, a good-looking older woman, came in. Jamie recognised the woman, "This is Jemima Slater," said Julian King. "She has flying lessons." Another aircraft taxied to the area at the front of the clubhouse.

"That's the television film crew," said Jemima. "Are we having a drink, Julian? I need to relax, sweetie." She sauntered off to a bench seat.

"I want you to tidy the garden up when you come next week," said Julian, "It's getting untidy, and there will be filming of the clubhouse in two weeks. Can you do that for us?" Alan failed to respond. He wasn't keen on gardening.

"That's OK, I'll do it," Jamie pictured a flight as a reward.

"We did have a gardener," Julian explained. "He was an elderly chap, but he died in rather tragic circumstances."

"What happened to him?"

"Stepped off a bus while it was still moving and hit his head on a lamp post. He was killed instantly."

His experience cultivating the garden at the flying club gave Jamie a taste for gardening. He found it a peaceful occupation and decided to get into landscape gardening when he left school in the coming summer. Flying would take a back seat. The flying club had been a good experience, but the RAF was not for him. He didn't want to live a disciplined lifestyle.

Jamie and Alan spent a few more months going to the flying club. When no one else was in the clubhouse, they took advantage of the bar, and the Bells Whisky became a favourite tipple of both the lads. A downside was that the flights didn't continue, and the offer of a flying scholarship was never mentioned again. Things had changed, and people were somewhat distant from them.

One Saturday, when Julian King saw Jamie washing the glass he had just used, he took the two cadets into his office. "You two boys have been helping yourselves to our supply of whisky. Now I'm not going to do anything about this. I won't say anything to get you into trouble because what you have done reminds me of what I used to be like when I was a teenager, a bit loose-brained. Anyway, today is your last day with us. Have a good future, boys. You can go now."

Jamie left school and applied for a place at Moreton Morrell Agricultural College. He was accepted after his successful exam results at school and his interview at the college. His father gave him his spade, the old one he had restored when he was a young man. "It'll serve you well, son," said his father, thinking ahead to when Jamie would strike out on his own as a landscape gardener at the end of his training at Moreton Morrell.

Chapter 40

1975-1985

Moreton Morrell and Worcester

Moreton Morrell is a village in one of the ancient Hundreds of Warwickshire, known as the Kington Hundred. From the time of Norman England, the village has been comprised of the village of Moreton and the hamlet of Morrell.

Jamie Watts rented a bedsit in the village. He subsidised the cost of the rent and the provision of spending money by working as a barman at a local pub. Applying himself seriously to his course at the agricultural college, Jamie realised that, with the small size of the room he rented, unused things he brought with him took up too much space.

"Can you take a few items back with you, Dad? Don't get rid of them; I just need the space," Jamie suggested on one of Ross and Laura's monthly visits. So the belongings, including the spade Ross gave Jamie, went to the house in Worcester where Laura and Ross moved to after retirement.

After the three years of his course, which he passed in 1980 with average grades, Jamie moved back in with his parents. He went into the garage and sorted through the items they stored while he was at college and decided to give them to the Oxfam charity shop.

While at Moreton Morrell College, Jamie concluded that agriculture and landscaping were not for him. He was still interested in aircraft but hadn't the confidence to get involved with flying. A ground-staff job at an airport would be the way to go, so Jamie began reading the Worcester Evening News classifieds. As a temporary measure, he got a job at Ye Olde Talbot, a traditional coaching inn near the town centre.

Not now having the arduous study task he had with his college course in Moreton Morrell, Jamie threw considerable energy and enthusiasm into his work at Ye Olde Talbot. The landlord noticed this, and as a result, Jamie was promoted to shift manager. He was content with his current job because he could do the shift, go home and forget work.

His interest in aircraft lingered in a simple way. He liked the sound of aircraft piston engines, notably the Rolls-Royce Merlin. But modern aircraft impressed him as well. He heard from one of the regular customers in Ye Olde Talbot that Concorde would fly from Elmdon Airport, heading for Paris. With its futuristic shape, the history-making aircraft was too good an opportunity to miss. So on the 16th of September, 1980, Jamie and his girlfriend, Donna French, headed for Elmdon Airport in his Austin Healey Sprite.

There was a long queue of traffic going into the airport car park, so when Jamie and Donna walked to the wire fence overlooking the runway, Concorde was slowly taxiing toward the take-off point. When it turned, the sleek shape, sideways on, caught the sunlight, and its beauty caused some in the crowd to gasp in amazement. Some minutes passed, and then the aircraft's four Rolls Royce Snecma Olympus 593 turbojet engines hit full throttle. The plane rapidly gained speed, hurtling down the runway. Its front undercarriage wheel lifted, and the rear wheels were soon off the ground. Then, as she drew parallel to where Jamie and Donna were standing, the Concorde, with afterburners blazing, was airborne. Many of the electronic alarms in the nearby parked cars burst into life with the concussive movement of air.

Very quickly, the beautiful machine became just a speck in the sky. The crowd was surprisingly silent, and the racket from the alarms caused people to quickly drift away to see if their car alarms had been activated.

"That was something else," said Jamie, as he and Donna walked hand-in-hand back to the Austin Healey. He looked at her. She was smiling. The sun glinted on her copper-auburn-coloured hair, and he realised again how beautiful she was. She squeezed his hand.

"What shall we do now?" she asked.

"How about a drink," he suggested. "I know a very nice pub near here. It's ancient, half-timbered, and we could get a meal too. It's called The Bear, and it's in Berkswell, a village not far from here."

"That sounds lovely; let's go."

On his break during the next shift at the Talbot, Jamie was chatting with one of the bartenders, Gary Stone. Jamie was telling him about the Concorde experience at Elmdon.

"I used to live in Solihull," said Gary. "I don't know whether you'll believe this, but I'll tell you what happened anyway. It was bizarre." Gary went quiet. The restroom upstairs was quiet, too.

"It was one Saturday afternoon," Gary began. "I'd been to The Malt Shovel, a pub on the A45, for a meal with a couple of friends. We were in my car, and I had just turned into Damson Parkway. Try to picture this, Jamie. On each side of the road, there are tall hedges with fields stretching out behind them. It was me who spotted the thing first," Gary stopped and glanced at Jamie, uncertain about whether or not to carry on.

"Come on, don't leave me in suspense."

"OK. Remember, what I'm going to tell you was witnessed by the three of us. As I turned the corner, over in the field to the left, about thirty feet in the air, was a UFO, silverish in colour, with very dark grey cones around the middle, the top and the bottom. I stopped to look at it briefly, but the road was busy, and we had to move on."

"You are joking."

"I'm not. As true as I'm sitting here, it happened, and as I said, three of us can vouch for it."

A few days later, Gary Stone's two friends, a young married couple, came into the Talbot. He invited them over to have a meal after his shift, and they confirmed to Jamie that the UFO incident happened.

Chapter 41

1986-2004

Westcliffe University, Worcester

The Oxfam shop had just opened one Saturday morning in 1986 when Doctor Marianne Dewis walked by. Being an avid reader of crime fiction, she was always on the hunt for paperbacks by Agatha Christie. The problem was that they were popular and a rarity to find.

She had browsed halfway along the middle shelf and had found a copy of Peril at End House. There was a noise in the back room where two people were sorting out donated goods. A clanging noise occurred, and then "Oh damn, damn, damn," was spoken by an angry female. "This damn spade, I'm fed up with it."

"I found it the other day when we moved our settee. Don't know how long it's been there. Let's put it in the shop. I'll put a label on it. How much do you think?"

"Ten p."

"No, come on, it's worth more than that."

Marianne stepped back and glanced to the back room where the two women were assessing the spade. She liked the look of it.

"Two pounds. I'll give you two pounds for it," Marianne called out. The two other women were startled by the voice that had joined the conversation. But then the woman who nearly tripped over the spade entered into the humour.

"Done," she called out. "Sold to the customer with a book in her hand." She brought the spade out and leaned it against the counter

"This does look interesting." Marianne was a lecturer at Westcliffe University, Worcester, in the department of Plant Biosciences. She was used to using tools smaller than a spade, tools associated with microscopic work. But spades were interesting. They had to do with soil, the growing medium that enabled her doctorate in plant life to exist.

"That's two pounds and twenty-five p, Madam."

Marianne fished around in her purse and paid. She lifted the spade. It was weighty and covered in dust. A good rub over would put it right.

During her time at the university, Marianne had put her heart into her job. She always went the added mile, but there was a long-standing problem in the laboratory with the overbearing attitude of its head, Professor Hinks. So Marianne intended to use the spade to challenge the issue.

"What the hell's that doing here?" shouted Professor Hinks. He saw the spade leaning against the desk where an electron microscope was being used by a student. Hinks took his station in life as a professor far too seriously. As was typical, his approach to Marianne was discourteous and rude, and her students overheard the tirade.

"I'm going to put it in a showcase on the wall there," she pointed to the place. "It'll help show the progression of agriculture over the years. I intend to have a series of agricultural tools, including a tractor, in a museum."

"Do you indeed? You can forget that idea, my girl."

"I am not *your* girl Professor; you can forget *that* idea." The students started laughing. "If you intend to be bullying and rude, let's do it in your damn office now." She got up so quickly her chair fell over. Hinks stepped back in surprise. Normally people cow-towed to him.

Marianne went to Hinks, grabbed his arm and marched him to his office. The students watched the performance as she led the way in and slammed the door behind them.

"Sit down," she said firmly, standing arms-akimbo. Hinks had gone pale. He sat.

"Get this straight, you horrible little man. Do not speak to me like that again in the presence of students. You can do so here. I may retaliate, as is my right. I accept that it is your right to advise about how the lab is run, but never go about it like you did a minute back."

"I apologise," he said meekly.

Marianne smiled. "Accepted, but don't worry, I was testing the water. The spade can go into the storage area."

Professor Patrick Hinks looked utterly bewildered.

"So it was all a game, suggesting a museum in our laboratory?"

"It was. Now I must apologise. We need to create a level playing field in our lab. I appreciate your work, but there would be better progress if respect was shown to everyone involved in the research."

"I take your point, Marianne. I'll do my best."

And so he did. After the confrontation, the research work flourished. Marianne took her spade down to the stores. "Look after it for me, Bob," she told the storekeeper. "I may need it someday soon."

* * *

After her onslaught on the abusive Professor Patrick Hinks, Doctor Marianne Dewis became loved by students and staff. She gained a professorship and was progressive in her role, ensuring each department was equipped with the latest equipment. She was coming for retirement at the end of the 2004 academic year. She wanted to create a lasting memorial of her presence as Vice Chancellor at Westcliffe.

She proposed her idea at a meeting of the Board of Governors and the Executive Team. "It will be an annual prize-giving to celebrate the achievement of the most forward-looking thesis in the academic year, awarded after results are announced."

"And it must be called the Dewis Prize-giving," suggested her second-in-command.

"But a different award each year. An award thought the most appropriate for the subject matter of the student winning the prize," Marianne added. The proposal was seconded and passed unanimously.

The winner of the Dewis Prize at its first ceremony was Philip Hendry, who obtained a first-class master's degree in Biological Plant Sciences. He had shone academically, and his research thesis was ground-breaking in a quirky sense. His aptitude for the applied science of plant microbiology was innovative, and the information, so logically presented, was close to Marianne's heart. "What ought we to award him, Marianne?" asked the Biosciences Head of Department.

She thought for a minute and smiled.

Chapter 42

2004-2009

Alfred Back

Alfred Back was born in Kenilworth. He was a gentle person who possessed that rare, old-fashioned desire to show consideration for his neighbours. He considered other people and respected their differences. *They're only human,* he would say, if an acquaintance felt aggrieved by another's comments.

Alf's occupation was that of a labourer on a farm near the village of Honiley, where he lived. Over the years, he developed many skills and often did jobs for friends and neighbours without charging them for his work.

Alf was happily married to Beverly. He and Bev had three adult children, two girls and a boy, who were also married. When the grandchildren visited, Nan and Grandpa Back delighted them with fuss and fun that they gave generously.

High Moat Farm was named after its proximity to The Pleasance, an island of relaxation in medieval times, reached by boat from Kenilworth Castle. Alf had worked at High Moat Farm for forty-nine years, and, whatever the weather, he had cycled to and from work. He was a valued worker, held in high esteem by the owners of the arable farm of two hundred and three acres. So valued was Alfred that the owners, Pete and Susan Smythe, at times of yearly celebration, invited the Back family to share the occasion.

The house and other buildings at High Moat Farm were situated on the higher part of a gentle slope leading down to an area of ancient woodland. When new workers started at High Moat, Pete Smythe introduced them to Alfred, who would ease them into their new job.

He would walk the new workers around the farm, its high pastures and lower wooded edges, telling them of the farm and the local countryside's history. In a sense, he *fused* them into the place and made them feel part of it. Generally, because of his introduction style, the workers felt attuned to their surroundings and gave their best.

On a July Monday of 2005, a man in his late twenties began work at High Moat. He was introduced to Alfred, who began his usual introductory tour of the land, and the pair got talking. Philip Hendry was on a gap year after finishing his course at Westcliffe University in Worcester. He wanted to get back to basics, nothing high-powered, as would befit his Master's degree.

They began to walk down the track toward dense woodland at the bottom of the hill. "What did you study?" Alf asked,

"Molecular Biology, but with a leaning toward Plant Science. Rather odd, really, but with the current need to fill the bellies of the starving in the third world, I wanted to understand what was needed to do that most efficiently."

"Did you come to any conclusions?"

"Interesting question. The answer is summarised in a gardening phrase that's been bandied about for years. Do you remember Gardeners Question Time when Percy Thrower used to say, *The answer lies in the soil?*"

"I remember it well. My favourite program."

"There's more truth in those words that can be imagined, but the understanding will only be recognised when people allow themselves to forget old gardening rules."

"What do you mean?"

"You know about double-digging?"

"Of course I do."

"And look at this field . . . how it is ploughed ready for seeding." Phil pointed to the field on the right of the track.

"I can't see anything wrong with the field."

"Yes, that's the problem. The soil of that field, any soil, for that matter, has millions upon millions of micro-organisms in it. Here's the point, if the organisms aren't disturbed, in other words, if the soil isn't ploughed or dug, it will give a better production yield. This has been proved by rigorous trials."

"Has it?" Alf found it difficult to believe.

"Indeed it has. Soil was designed to operate at full efficiency if all of its micro-organisms are disturbed as little as possible."

"How do we leave it undisturbed when we need to plant it up with crops? For example, this field is going to be planted with cabbage. It needs to be ploughed before planting. How is it possible to leave it undisturbed?"

"Let's say as undisturbed as possible. It is done by layering it with compost. That process generates the ideal bacterial conditions for plant growth and softens the soil beneath."

"I can't see that myself. All my life, I have dug, double-dug and ploughed. And think of how much compost it would take to cover that field," Alf pointed.

"Admittedly, that need would have to be addressed. But think of this. With any new, large-scale working method, the changes to make the process work efficiently doesn't take place overnight. Time will tell, Alf. Give the method

I've told you time to gain recognition, maybe a few years, and it'll come to the fore, you mark my words."

They came to a wide opening in the hedge that led into a field to their left. As they neared the opening, they heard the sound of a swarm of bees. They walked past it on the far right of the track to be safe.

"I heard you did well at college. You won a prize as a result of your research?"

"I did. It's a prize that recognises the value of a student's research. I won the prize because of the value of the research into soil conditions I just told you about."

"What did you win?"

Phil laughed. "Well, each year, there's a different prize. The prize depends on the nature of the research and how valuable it is for the population."

"So, what did you win?" Alf repeated.

"What I won was well-intentioned, but it shows that some of the competition's organisers didn't get the full point of my research, that digging is out of date."

"Digging's out of date? You must be joking. So, what did you win?"

"A spade."

Alf laughed.

"I brought it with me. Thought a spade might be useful in my new job. Judging by the shape, it's quite old. I'll show you when we get back to the canteen."

* * *

"That's a nice tool," said Alfred when Phil handed him the spade. "And I think you're right; it's quite old. See the curved shape of the spade part? That's not the usual style of a spade these days."

"Do you like it?"

"Like it? I'll say I like it."

"It's yours."

Alf stepped back. "But I can't do that." He offered the spade back to Phil.

"I think you deserve it more than I do, Alfie. It needs to go to someone whose livelihood is related to digging. Remember what I said, that they got it wrong when I was awarded a spade for trying to tell the world to stop digging." Phil Hendry pushed the spade back to Alf.

"Have it with my compliments."

There was another reason why Phil gave the spade to his new friend. Alfred reminded him of his father, who died when Phil was eleven.

"Thank you, son; I'll treasure this," Alf said. He sat down and held the spade close.

On High Moat Farm, ditches and culverts, strategically placed for drainage of the fields, led downhill to a stream which flowed toward Kenilworth Castle. Maintenance of the drainage took place yearly in late April. Although Alf had started to feel his age, he was determined to join the event. From Alfred's viewpoint, it was a yearly ritual that ushered in the spring, with leaf buds and flowers emerging in a riot of life and energy.

But there was a problem. At one time, Alfred, with almost boundless energy, could continue physical work for an entire ten-hour shift; now, he needed to stop and rest every so often to ease his tired muscles.

"You need to retire, Dad," his eldest son often said. Beverly noticed Alf was arriving home on his cycle from High Moat Farm later these days. And now, although the meal was prepared that they would eat together and chat, he would sit in his chair and fall asleep.

"Why don't you do as David suggests, dear," Bev said, hoping he would take notice of those who could see the effects of his age. "You need to retire and ease off a bit," she said. But he was stubborn.

"You are the love of my life, Alfred Back," said Bev on the evening Phil Hendry gave him the spade. "You're later than usual," she spoke more firmly. She had been worried. Every few minutes, she stood by the window, looking down the lane, wishing to see him cycling home.

"I'll be alright, love. Now that better weather's coming, I'll get my energy back. You wait and see."

He arrived at High Moat the next day, put his sandwiches on the top shelf of his locker, and grasped his spade. "Thank you for this, Phil," he called into the next room, where he could see Phil Hendry sitting, conversing with the other farm workers over a cup of tea. Phil waved.

"Are you going to be alright with the work today, Alf," asked Steve Spiers, the foreman. Alf was determined to be alright clearing the ditches. He always was, and it was the start of spring. He looked out of the window at the blue sky.

"'Course I'm alright. What makes you think I'm not?"

"OK, then let's get going," the foreman said, and they all sauntered off to begin work.

The drainage ditch started after the wide entry to the twenty-acre Top field. It continued to where the track did a sharp left-hand turn, where a culvert took the drainage water under the track and into the stream.

Alfred scrambled into the ditch with his new spade, determined to combat the idea that he could no longer do the work. He drove the spade into the bottom of the trench and slung the mud onto the bank. Alfred's hearing, not being as good as it was a few years back, failed to hear the shout from Phil Hendry to "Get out, Alf."

The others ran down toward the woodland. Alf felt the first sting when they began to run. He looked up. The sky had been the clear blue he loved; now, it was dark and noisy as the swarm descended on him.

Phil Hendry didn't give a damn about the bees. As the swarm descended on Alfred and the other workers ran out of danger, Phil Hendry leapt to Alfred's side in the ditch. Phil began to feel the pain of the attack, but regardless, he grabbed Alf's arm and scrambled out of the gulley. Pulling Alfred up, he hoisted him onto his shoulders in a fireman's lift and ran, as best he could, down the slope to the stream at the bottom. As he leapt into it and he and Alf were immersed, the bees dispersed.

Phil surfaced and pulled Alfred half onto the bank. He cleared debris from the stream away from Alf's nose and mouth. He saw red spots on the older man's skin all around his face and neck.

"Get here quick," he shouted. "Help get him out." Strong arms pulled Alf out of the stream and onto the bank.

Exhausted by the exercise, Phil dragged himself out of the stream and went to Alf. He felt for his pulse, but there was none. Leant close to Alf's mouth and nose for a sign of breathing and realised, with the sorrow he felt when his father died, that his new friend, who had a most generous nature, had died.

Chapter 43

2015

Intermission

How the years have flown by. People's lives and loves have come and gone like a mist that rises and is here for a little while and then disappears. If only our lives and loves could last forever.

So many events have occurred since the fiery young man, Thomas Satchwell, formed his spade on a tilt-hammer at the forge mill in Halveston, on the bank of the Stour.

Sometimes the World has seen golden years of peace and happiness for many whilst, at the same time, there has been turmoil and a struggle for survival for others. In our little lives, fathers have handed down their tools to their sons. A chisel has been used to form a mortice joint a hundred and fifty years after it was used to do the same task by an ancestor.

Mothers and aunts have shown daughters and nieces how to knit two, purl two . . . K2, P2. *Do this, my dear; it's called rib.* And the stitches are counted, the rows lovingly forming a little hat for a newborn baby with knitting needles used by a great-grandmother.

"Dad."

"Yes, son?" the father asked.

"You know I'm eight years old, and you are thirty-one."

"That's right."

"Thirty-one is old. How can we slow the years down, dad, so we have more time together before you die?"

It was an ongoing process for the father, learning how to answer such intriguing questions. But it was a good thought, a wise thought from a young mind. If only that could be done. A vast extension to the length of life so that we could spend countless years with our loved ones.

But we come to a time at High Moat Farm when the field has been ploughed, ready for a new crop. It was early spring, and ditches needed clearing again from mud and debris.

The team of workers arrived at the wide entrance to Twenty Acre Top. Terry Ennis, an eighteen-year-old assigned to start work at the upper part of the ditch, slid down the steep bank into the gulley.

Over the years, the drainage ditches, as happens with streams and watercourses, are eroded by the passage of water. This had happened to the ditch at the side of Twenty Acre Top.

"Hey, look at this," shouted Ennis. So the others stopped work and went to see what he had found.

"It's only an old spade, said one of the others. "Someone must have forgotten it."

Terry looked at the implement. He liked the shape of the spade, and he wiped the mud off its surface on the nearby grass. At the end of his shift Terry, being a conscientious young man, left the spade in the hedge, hanging it on a branch of hazel, just in case its owner came looking for it.

Springtime went on apace and turned into full summer when branches grew longer on the hedges and trees, and foliage flourished. The spade inside the growing hedge was lost to sight as the years passed.

Chapter 44

2021

The Tipperary Walk and a Discovery

The early autumn day dawned bright, clear and full of promise. The previous few days had been a mix of overcast skies and torrential rain. So Rob, his wife Alexandra, who Rob called Alex, and their son, Christopher, decided to take a walk to take advantage of the break in the weather. They drove to Kenilworth and parked in an area adjacent to Kenilworth Castle, opposite the Clarendon Arms, where, after the walk, they would go for a meal.

The walk started well. On Rob's suggestion, they deviated from their usual route, the lane at the side of the castle leading to the area called the Pleasance. Instead, they turned into fields on the right. It would be a five-mile walk taking in a variety of scenery and a quarter mile of the A462 road between Balsall Common and Kenilworth, on which lay the Tipperary Inn. The walk would be through a long stretch of woodland, go around the edge of numerous fields, and finish up at Kenilworth castle and inside The Clarendon Arms.

At first, the walk was easygoing. Alex, Chris and Rob passed the Tipperary Inn, once owned by Harry Williams, a co-writer of the First World War song, 'It's a Long Way to Tipperary', and then they entered the deeply wooded area.

The walk became treacherously muddy, caused by the path being a popular route used by folks doing horse riding. But the three struggled through the mud, ankle-deep in places and were thankful when they came out of the wood and onto more solid ground.

"Any idea how much further it is?" Alex asked.

"If I remember right, we're about halfway," said Rob.

Chris led on, setting a steady pace, and Rob thought of a time back in 1954 when the medical student, Roger Bannister, helped by his two pacemakers, Chris Brasher and Chris Chattaway, broke the four-minute mile record.

Rob looked at his son, another Chris, striding ahead as if setting the pace. "Hey, Chris, slow down," he called.

Alex looked back and smiled. "Come on, Rob. You can do it. Another half hour, and we'll be at the Clarendon."

Rob looked at the extent of the field they had just joined. He walked faster and took the lead. After rounding a bend, some farm buildings, a house, brick barns and stainless steel silage tanks came into view.

As they came to the buildings, the track was tarmacked. Then, after a sharp right-hand bend, the pathway went down a slope at the side of a long, newly ploughed field.

Rob was still in the lead. When they were halfway down the field, Chris called for him to stop. "Have you noticed something here?" he said. Rob turned to see what his son was on about. "Over there, look," Chris pointed to the newly cut hedgerow by the ditch, and then Rob saw it, a spade hanging on the branch of a tree on the other side of a ditch.

Rob scrambled into the ditch, which was not too muddy compared to the path they had taken through the wood. He reached up, grasped the spade and pulled, but it was hooked onto the branch and stayed in place.

"Give us a hand, Chris." Christopher, being six inches taller than Rob, had no trouble lifting the spade over a knob on the branch. He handed it to his father.

"Looks old," Rob said. "I wonder why it's there, on the tree?" He saw some indents on the front of the socket where the wooden handle was fitted into the steelwork. He rubbed some dried mud off the surface of the steel and saw the letters *T* and *S*.

Rob scrambled out of the ditch. "This is quite a find," he said, showing Alex. She touched the handle, which was surprisingly clean.

"Are you keeping it?"

"I am," Rob said. Then, with the spade resting on his shoulder, he and the others walked on through the Warwickshire countryside.

They arrived at their car. Rob put the spade in the boot and followed Alex and Chris as they strolled over to the Clarendon Arms, where they ordered a meal and sat in a quiet corner.

"D'you think the spade's very old?" Alex asked Rob.

"Going by the shape it is. Spades aren't made like that these days."

"Maybe we could do a bit of research on the internet," suggested Chris. "There's a clue about who made it with that T and S stamped into the metalwork."

Alex was deep in thought. "If that spade could talk," she said quietly to Rob and Chris, "I wonder what stories it would tell?"

The End

JJ Overton

J.J. Overton,
Coventry,
The West Midlands of England.

J.J. Overton is from Coventry, in England's industrial West Midlands. He served an apprenticeship as a precision toolmaker, studied mechanical engineering, and is a Freeman of the City of Coventry. He was assistant managing director of Grey and Rushton Precision Tools and subsequently was involved with quality control at industrial giants Alfred Herbert Machine Tools, Massey-Ferguson, and Courtaulds Structural Composites. In later years, before devoting more time to writing, he was a self-employed stained glass artist. His native Warwickshire, with its rich, and sometimes turbulent history, influences his writing. He is married and has two adult sons.

Printed in Great Britain
by Amazon